SLEIGH ALL THE WAY

A HOLIDAY ROMANCE NOVEL
BOOK 7

AMANDA SIEGRIST

Short Stories

Paint By Murder

Follow Me, Sweet Darling

Sleighville Novel

Dashing Through the Fear

Here Comes Chaos

The Last Noel

Standalone Novel

The Danger with Love

Conquering Fear Novel

Co-written with Jane Blythe

Drowning in You

Out of the Darkness

Closing In

MERRY CHRISTMAS.

MAY YOUR DAYS AND NIGHTS BE FILLED WITH HOLIDAY CHEER!

1

"I HATE CHRISTMAS."

"Eww. Hate is a strong word. You should say dislike."

Serenity rolled her eyes at her sister, Opal. She would *not* say dislike because it wasn't a strong enough word. She hated Christmas. Despised it.

Not that she'd confess that to anyone but her sister. It was their little secret, and she planned to keep it that way. She didn't understand why Opal didn't hate it too. They both had such a good reason for it. There was no way she'd ever let her boys know she didn't like the holiday they adored. Though they were thirteen and growing so quickly into young men, she didn't want to take the spirit of Christmas away. That wouldn't be fair to them. Not that they believed in Santa Claus anymore. That ended when they were nine. But they still loved everything that Christmas entailed. The thought of Santa, the goodies, the decorations, the cheer, the presents, of course.

"You're also cheating. You're not supposed to buy cookies," Opal continued in the bossy way she'd perfected since their childhood. Being the older sister, she was way too good at it. Serenity never could get her to stop or fight back.

Serenity stuck out her tongue as she drew another frosted sugar cookie out of the container and onto a plate painted with elves. Her boys wouldn't find it odd she hadn't made any cookies. It was for the best that she didn't. She and baking did not get along—at all. She'd burned more cookies in her life than she cared to remember.

"My boys love the treats from Lynn's bakery. It's not cheating when I'm buying them the best."

Opal pursed her lips, her eyes crinkled as if contemplating arguing with that statement, then nodded and smiled. "I can't argue with that. She has magic in her hands." Then Opal snatched a cookie and chomped into it with vigor.

"So, dickface call yet?"

Serenity didn't hide the disgusting tremble that coated her body at the thought of even talking to Eric, the boys' father.

"No, do you honestly think he will?"

Because she was wise enough to know that Eric, though he claimed to be the best father in the world, was fooling no one. Not even the boys. Eric had let them down so many times, they hardly asked about their father anymore. It was sad more than anything. Of course, she didn't want to be the parent that didn't make an effort, the one who would look like the bad person, even when she wasn't anywhere close to that. She reached out to Eric more than he deserved. Every time, he said he'd be there, and every time, he failed on his promises.

"Christmas is in a few weeks."

As if Serenity needed reminding. She hadn't started shopping for Christmas presents—for anyone. The boys were the most important. Yet she didn't even want to think about going into the crazy, busy stores and buying things they'd play with for a week and then forget about. Though they were getting older and not into toys much. They were glued to their gaming station more often than not, or outside playing some kind of sport. She couldn't complain about that. She adored that they loved being outdoors and not attached to an electronic device, like their cell phones.

"If Eric doesn't care about that, why should I?"

"I agree, but we both know you'll end up calling him anyway and trying for those boys."

That was the truth. She tried so hard for them, and Eric never showed an ounce of care. Some days, she wished he never existed in their lives at all.

Opal finished her cookie, swiping her hands clean of the crumbs. "So why do we hate Christmas today?"

As if she needed a new reason every day. But her sister knew her so well. Only two years apart, they were as close as two sisters could be. Almost as if they had been twins, like her boys were. Sometimes, people even said they looked alike, asking if they were indeed twins. Serenity always took it as a compliment. Opal always had the look of murder on her face, though she could never figure out why, and she never bothered to ask. Some things were better not knowing.

"Royce reminded me this morning that the second annual snowman building contest is next weekend in Mulberry. Remember, they won last year. I am not looking forward to doing it again. I'm pretty sure I hurt my back last year and can still feel the kink I twisted in my lower back. Being on my hands and knees for so long sucks."

"But you know you'll sign up and rock that shit like you always do."

Serenity closed the empty plastic container and set it on the counter behind her to put in the recycling bin later. The plate looked pretty as she headed out of the kitchen to the dining room and set the beautifully decorated sugar cookies in the middle of the table. When the boys got home from school, delicious treats would be waiting for them. After they finished their homework, of course.

"Why don't you join our team this year?"

Opal, who had followed her into the room, laughed so hard, Serenity knew the answer before she even spoke.

"I'm not freezing my ass off to build a snowman. You know me better than that."

Oh, she did. Serenity could handle the cold. She was forced to be outside more times than she cared to because the boys loved sledding and started snowboarding last year. No matter how many times she tried to talk her sister into joining the fun, she always found an excuse to get out of it.

"Why not ask Cam? I'm sure he'd jump at the chance."

No, that would be a bad idea.

"I'm sure he's busy."

"That man would jump off a bridge for you."

She smiled, hoping she could hide the terror of the thought from her sister, but knew she failed. She walked away to the kitchen, though she knew that didn't mean the conversation was over.

"You invited him to the family Christmas party, right?"

Serenity turned on the hot water, flicking her fingers under the liquid until she found the right temperature, then plugged the sink. After adding dish soap, she swished the water to create suds. She didn't have to hand-wash the dishes because they had a dishwasher. But she needed something to occupy her mind while her sister continued to get on her nerves. This was not a subject she wanted to breach. She'd preferred talking about the dreaded holiday coming up, and she hated it with a passion. So that said enough.

"We're friends. I'm not inviting him to the party. Everyone in the family will think we're more than friends."

"You could be more than friends."

No. No, she couldn't. Because it would ruin everything between them. They had to remain friends, no matter what.

She'd met Cam last year around Christmastime. The first time had been a random meeting. He stopped her on the sidewalk when she had been leaving the floral shop, picking up some poinsettias to bring to her parents and congratulating her on winning the snowman contest. It'd been so long since a man showed any interest in her, she screwed up the whole interaction. She chalked it up to nerves and tried to forget about the entire incident. Then she saw him again at Theresa and Aiden's New Year's Eve party and managed to salvage her first horrible greeting with him. From there, they became friends.

He was handy with just about anything. She'd called him more times than not to fix this or that around the house. He was wonderful with her boys. Playing baseball and football with them in the summer. More times than their own father ever had. She liked having him around. Too much sometimes.

But if she indulged in even a moment of things progressing into more than friends, everything would fall apart. It always did. No relationship she had ever turned out in a happily ever after. Maybe that said something was wrong with her, not the guy. While she liked Cam—more than she should—she didn't want to lose him from her life.

"What are you so afraid of?" Opal asked when Serenity never responded.

"Nothing. We're friends. He has never given me any indication he's wanted more with me."

That was not a lie. He had never asked her out. Not once. There were times she swore he might. The way he looked at her. So focused and intense. Eyeing her lips like he wanted to lean in closer. Yet he never did. He never said, "Hey, let me take you out to dinner." Heaven help her, she would've caved and said yes.

But since he hadn't, she'd had time to fortify her resolve. If he asked, she'd deny him and they'd remain friends and all would be well in her world.

"That man looks at you like he wants to bone you so hard."

Serenity snorted and shook her head. "Stop. He does not."

"You look at him in the same way. Ask him to the party."

"No."

Opal grinned at her wickedly. "Okay, I'll ask him then."

"Why? It's a family Christmas party. You know how crazy they get." Serenity turned around from the sink. She'd been standing there with her hands sitting in the soapy water and not actually washing any dishes. She wasn't fooling anyone, especially her sister.

"Consider it my Christmas present to you. I'm going to help you get that man in bed. Bone him hard. For me."

Serenity couldn't stop another snort, pressing her lips together to stop the smile that wanted to break free. "I'm not sleeping with him. And I hate Christmas presents, remember? Don't get me anything."

"It's my Christmas goal this year. Deal with it. And when you're done, I want all the details. All the dirty, juicy details. He is such a fine man."

Another truth she couldn't deny. He was more than fine. He was everything she always wanted in a guy.

If only she weren't so afraid to open her heart one more time.

They had to remain friends. Nothing else was acceptable.

A SOLID BANG on the door startled him, making him jump and his hand slip, chipping a piece of wood off he hadn't meant to chip—and a small little cut on his hand as well. When the door swung open and Mase walked in, Cam stifled a groan and forced out a grin, ignoring the slight pain in his finger. A little blood and pain never got in the way when he was working. He'd cut himself more times than he cared to remember. All part of the job.

It didn't matter how wide he smiled, Mase, who he'd been friends with for over ten years, knew his moods well. One grin wasn't going to hide his irritation. Not only at messing up his project and being interrupted but also at how his day was going in general.

"What's wrong?"

Cam turned his attention back to the project in front of him and shrugged. "It's been that kind of day." He rubbed his finger over his pants, wiping some of the blood off. It wasn't a deep cut. He could find a band-aid, but he didn't think it was necessary. A small graze, if anything.

Mase winced when he came up behind Cam. "I didn't mean to knock so hard on the door. I can smooth that out for you."

Of course, he was talking about the visible nick in the wood that he'd taken out with the chisel. Mase knew he'd never nick it so bad on purpose. It didn't take a mind reader to know how it'd happened.

"It's fine. I got it."

It would also help him to work out the frustration that'd been building for far too long. A little bit of sanding and a bit more chiseling and he'd be done.

And hopefully on his way to impressing the one woman who was the most difficult to impress. Nothing he ever did got him out of the dreaded friend zone he had seemed to land himself in last New Year's Eve.

"What's up?" Cam backed away from the piece and headed over to the mini fridge he kept in his workshop. It was almost identical to the workshop Mase had as well. A small couch with a TV against the wall for when he wanted to take a break. A mini fridge with beer, pop, and water for any occasion. And, of course, his workbench and the multitude of tools he needed for any kind of wood project he might want to work on. "Beer?"

Mase nodded and leaned against the worktable behind him, staring at the project Cam had been working on tirelessly for the past few months. A few more touchups and he'd be done.

He twisted the cap off two bottles, handed one to Mase, and took a large gulp of his own.

"Life's been so busy with Hope running for mayor that I haven't been to visit in a while. I didn't know you were working on something so big. I don't remember taking this contract either. Who's it for?"

Cam leaned against the worktable next to his longtime best friend and business partner. It would make sense for Mase to know any contract he took, just as he'd know about any that Mase took on. Unlike last year when they were slammed with too many kitchen projects right before

Christmas, this year they weren't as busy. By choice. They wanted an easier holiday. Less stress. More time for family and fun. With Mase recently engaged to Hope and finding a property in Mulberry to begin building a home for them, they needed a break from working so much.

His eyes zoned in on every little detail of the sleigh he'd built from scratch. From the bench to sit on, to the walls to hold it together, to the intricate wooden blades on the bottom that would pull it through the snow with ease. He'd carved and cut and put it all together with his own two hands. Sweated and hurt himself too many times to count, yet it was all worth it.

Because when Serenity laid her eyes on it, she'd fall in love. With the sleigh and, hopefully, with him as well. For someone who loved Christmas as much as she did, how could she not love this handmade sleigh built for Santa himself?

"Cam?"

He took another pull of his beer. "I thought Serenity might like it."

Mase nodded before taking a sip of his beer. "She does love Christmas."

That's why Cam knew she'd love this present. She dolled up her house in so much Christmas cheer, it would fit right in. He'd helped her last weekend hang up all her Christmas lights on the house. As it was a two-story house, it hadn't been easy getting the second level lit up, but he persevered. The bright smile that lit up her face when he finished was worth every mind-numbing moment of hanging off a ladder. He swore he was going to fall every other second. He wouldn't say he was afraid of heights, but it hadn't been a pleasant task.

"It's pretty big."

Cam turned to Mase. "Too big?"

Damn it. Why was Mase making him second-guess himself?

"Is it meant for riding or just display?"

It was meant for whatever the hell Serenity wanted to use it for. If she wanted to ride in it, he'd buy her a horse to pull it. Or rent one. There had to be a place around here somewhere where a person could rent a horse. Or whatever. He'd figure it out. He hadn't thought that far ahead. The idea popped into his head to build her a sleigh and that's what he had set out to do. It hadn't been cheap. Wood was so expensive at the moment. Yet it didn't matter. Nothing had but putting his hands to work and creating the beauty in front of him. As soon as he fixed the nick he created a few minutes ago and double-checked every other spot on the sleigh, it'd be done and ready to be delivered to her house.

"It's meant for her to enjoy however she wants to."

Mase set his hand on his shoulder and squeezed. "Good luck, man. You deserve happiness, and I like Serenity. She's great."

The only problem was she didn't see him as boyfriend material. He heard Mase's unspoken words, even if he didn't have the balls to say them out loud.

Since the moment he started chatting with her at the New Year's Eve party last year, he knew she was the one. Though their first meeting hadn't gone well at all, that night, it was as if it had never happened. They talked as if they'd known each other all their lives. Easy and smooth. Laughing and smiling. They clicked like he'd never clicked with another woman before. Even better than he had with his high school sweetheart that he thought he'd spend the rest of his life with—until she cheated on him with his best friend.

That opened his eyes. That made him more cautious and a lot more hesitant with women.

Perhaps that was his problem now. He kept his distance so much, Serenity didn't know he wanted to be more than friends.

Well, no more. He was fixing that issue starting with this amazing present that would open her eyes wide and clear. A friend didn't make such an extravagant gift. No. Only a man interested in more would do something like that.

He hoped she saw it that way anyway. With his luck, he'd still be stuck in the same rut with her, and he didn't know how much longer he'd survive if that happened.

Of course, he knew. He'd survive for as long as it took because she was worth the wait. She was worth everything in this world.

"Is it too much?"

He'd been so sure this was the right move. Now Mase had him rethinking everything.

"It's perfect, man. She shouldn't doubt how you feel after she sees this."

That was the hope.

He chugged the rest of his beer, his eyes staring so hard at the sleigh in front of him, they started to blur.

Mase wasn't fully correct. It wasn't quite perfect just yet.

But it'd get there. He didn't care how many more cuts and bruises he got, he'd make it the damn best sleigh there ever was.

2

_____

THE LAUNDRY BASKET made a loud popping sound when she let it drop to the floor at the foot of her bed. She strained her ears, wanting to make sure she heard what she thought she had correctly.

Yep.

Besides the front door slamming, so had another door. Presumably to a bedroom.

Sighing, she left her room with the knowledge she wouldn't be getting back to folding the laundry anytime soon. Nothing new there. It was an excellent day if she managed to fold and put away clothes on the same day she washed them. Clearly, today wasn't going to be one of those days.

She found Royce in the dining room already munching on one of the cookies she had set out for them, his notebook open and his math book as well.

"What happened?"

She decided to ignore the fact he had already grabbed a cookie. It wouldn't matter if Randall did either. They were both great about doing their homework right away before playing around.

Since Randall wasn't in the room, he had to be the culprit for slamming doors. Royce wouldn't look at her.

He shrugged. "Kids picking on him again on the bus. Bunch of jerks."

It sat on the tip of her tongue to correct his language. Not that calling someone a jerk was a complete swear word, but she didn't raise her boys to be rude and call people names. Nothing left her mouth because anyone who picked on her boys *was* a jerk. They deserved to be called a lot worse.

Randall was the quieter of her boys. Shy, more reserved. Royce was always by his side, making sure he was included and didn't revert into his shell too much.

"Which kids?"

Royce still wouldn't look at her. "I don't know, Mom."

"You do know. You don't want to tell me."

He didn't even try to suppress a sigh as he finally turned his gaze toward her. "Last time you talked to the bus company, nothing happened. The school doesn't care either."

Well, then she'd go right to the source. The parents.

"Was it Dawson again?" She forced herself not to slam a hand to her hip as if she were berating and hollering at Royce. Because she wasn't. She only wanted to know who was picking on her boys.

Royce knew how patient she could be. They'd yet to win a war against her. And they never would. He knew it.

"Yeah, it's always him. He was calling him names like dickwad and loser. *Ran, ran as fast as you can*," Royce said in a mocking tone, reciting what Dawson had been saying to Randall.

How unoriginal. And bad grammar. Trying to make it rhyme like it would make it even funnier or something. Kids could be so cruel.

Though Royce had said some kids were picking on Randall, she knew that Dawson was the instigator and the others just followed his lead. *He* was the bully.

Serenity walked up to Royce, hugging him as best as she could since he didn't stand up. Though he tried to pretend he didn't want the hug, he leaned into her, telling her how much he needed it anyway.

"We'll order pizza tonight. How does that sound?"

"Can I have another cookie?"

She ruffled his hair. "Of course, you can."

Then she left the room to talk to Randall. She thought about knocking on the door first but decided against it. He'd mumble she couldn't enter and that wasn't happening. He was sitting at his desk, his head down, his shoulders slumped.

She walked up behind him and gave him an awkward hug. Unlike Royce, who didn't turn and insist on a better hug, Randall did. He shifted until he was in her arms, his head pressed tight to her stomach.

"I'll take care of this. It's not okay for someone to hurt you like that."

Randall didn't say anything, though he usually didn't. That's why she always interrogated Royce instead. He was more likely to give her the information compared to Randall. He wanted to ignore it as if that would make it go away. Despite having every intention of calling the bus company and the school about this incident, she'd be having a chat with Dawson's parents as well.

When Randall pulled away after a few minutes of holding him, she gasped and gently touched his chin.

"He hit you!"

The cut on his lip said Dawson had.

Randall brushed her hand away and shook his head. "I tripped. Running."

"Randall...if he hit you..."

He shook his head more adamantly. "I tripped. I tripped like the loser I am."

"Oh, honey." She started to reach for him again, but he leaned away, a clear indication he didn't want to be coddled again. "You're not a loser. And he's jealous of you. Bullies always are."

And she figured that's why Dawson taunted that ridiculous saying ran, ran as fast as you can. Because Randall must've run off the bus, lost his footing, and tripped, hitting his mouth on the pavement. All she wanted to do was hug him tight, and he wanted to continue to pretend nothing happened.

"I have to finish my homework, Mom."

End of conversation.

For now, she'd let it go. Smothering him would only make him hide in his shell even more.

"I'm ordering pizza for supper. You want breadsticks too?"

"Yeah, sure," he mumbled, shrugging, his head buried in his math book as he had when she first walked in.

"There are cookies on the dining room table. Don't forget to grab one."

He nodded but didn't look at her.

She left him be, grabbing her phone and making calls immediately. She received the same spiel she got the last time from the bus company. They'd keep a closer eye on it and make sure Dawson didn't sit by Randall. That obviously wasn't working. Next, she called the school where she got the same response. They'd keep an eye on it and have a chat with the entire class about respecting each other and being nice. Yeah, that was going to fix the problem with ease. Not.

Randall wasn't likely to leave his room until she pried him from it when the pizza arrived. It broke her heart when these things happened. Made her feel helpless that she couldn't protect her kids from the cruelty of the world. She ruffled his hair and kissed his cheek when she told him she was going to order pizza and pick it up.

What she didn't tell him was she planned to make an extra stop along the way.

She told Royce the same thing, though when his gaze connected with hers, she knew he knew what else she was going to do.

"It won't make a difference."

"Nobody messes with my boys and doesn't get an earful. Don't ever forget that." She kissed the top of his head. "Keep the door locked and don't answer the door for anyone. Got it?"

"I know the routine, Mom."

Of course, he did, but it was her job to remind them each time anyway. She couldn't help herself. While she knew they were capable of staying home alone for a few hours now and again, it didn't mean it got easier to leave them.

She grabbed her purse, locked the door, and took a few deep, calming breaths before starting the car.

Dawson's mom and dad were about to get a rude awakening. She didn't relish it one bit. His father, Warren, worked at the local newspaper as the only editor. He was demanding, judgmental, and crass, and she didn't know anyone who liked him. Dawson's mother, Sharon, owned the only salon in town. Serenity had learned early on not to get her hair done there. Sharon was the worst gossip in town. At this moment, she was okay with that ugly trait. Because she wanted everyone in town to know what kind of mean, rude little boy they had. Though, she suspected, everyone already knew that. Because his parents were just as terrible.

When she was done, she'd get some pizza next door at the pizza joint. Then spend a relaxing evening at home with her boys. Maybe even challenge them in a game of Mario Kart. She was terrible at the game, but she knew it'd put a smile on their face and that's all she wanted.

Her phone ringing in her purse startled her. She let it fall silent, not wanting to dig for it while driving. It didn't take her long to make it into town. It was a small town and they didn't live far from the main drag.

One missed call from Cam.

Seeing his name made her heart palpitate in an unnatural rhythm. She listened to his voicemail. His strong, soothing voice made her wish for things she shouldn't. He had called to let her know he had a surprise for her. What kind of surprise? And why? Ugh. Hopefully, not a Christmas present. She still needed to do her shopping—for literally everyone—and she had no idea what to get Cam. The man had everything he needed.

Her eyes glided to the salon lit up with Christmas cheer on the outside and wanted to gag at the sight. First, from all the Christmas paraphernalia. Second, from the thought of what she had to do. She might fight to the death for her boys, but it didn't mean she enjoyed doing it.

One minor delay wouldn't hurt her.

She hit the dial button, and her heart skipped a beat when Cam answered on the first ring.

"Hey, how's it going?"

She smiled at his cheery voice, boxing it up to take out later because she knew this encounter would put her in a sour mood.

"Oh, I'm about to murder someone for hurting my son. How are you?"

CAM JERKED at Serenity's words. One, at the way she said it so merrily. Two, because they sounded so foreign coming out of her mouth. She had a fearsome wrath when it came to her boys, but murder? That sounded a little much for her.

"What happened? Can I help?"

Well, he wasn't offering to help murder someone, even though that's how it came out. Not that he thought she had been serious. Or had she?

No. That was silly. Serenity was the nicest, sweetest woman he'd ever met. She'd never hurt someone.

"Yeah, you want to hold them down while I pound the shit out of them?"

He chuckled, despite knowing she wasn't kidding. He could hear the pain in her voice.

"I can do that."

She started laughing herself. After a few hard chuckles, it turned into a sob.

He'd never heard her sound so distraught. She was always a happy, bubbly person. Helping others without hesitating, doing anything and everything for her boys, working two jobs, and volunteering whenever she had a chance. Being so busy, it was a surprise she didn't lose her cool more. It had to take a toll on her.

"Serenity, where are you?"

He heard her inhale deeply then let it out slowly. "I'm sitting in my car not far from the pizza place."

"I'll be right there."

"To help me or stop me?"

Not that he condoned violence, but he'd not only fallen in love with Serenity, he also loved those boys with all his heart. If she was so pissed she was ready to throw a punch, then it meant something bad happened. He'd help her in any way he could, including throwing a few of his own. As a very last resort, anyway. He didn't like violence at all.

"To support you in any way I can. Are the boys okay?"

She sniffed. "They are. Some kids are picking on Randall again. I've had enough. You don't need to come."

"And if I want to?"

His heart beat erratically, waiting for the rejection. For her to tell him to mind his own business. That he was only a friend and it wasn't his problem. Well, damn it, he wanted to make it his problem.

"Do you want to join us for pizza tonight?"

"I'd love that. I'll be right there. Wait for me."

"Bye, Cam."

The line went dead. He suspected she wasn't going to wait for him. He couldn't get mad about that because those boys weren't his and he had no right to tell her to wait. It didn't mean he wanted her to do it alone.

He grabbed his wallet and keys and flew out the door. His tires might've even squealed when he peeled out of the driveway. Thankfully, they hadn't had any snow yet this season, oddly enough. They'd had bad snowstorms in November more times than he could remember, and even rare ones in October. But he wasn't particularly fond of the snow, so it didn't bother him they hadn't had any snow yet this year. There was some in the forecast for next week. Hopefully, it changed by then.

Ten minutes later, he found an empty spot next to Serenity's car and saw her jabbing a finger in Sharon's face inside the salon. Oh, shit.

He rushed out of the truck and into the salon to hear Sharon's nasty words.

"I'm sure your boys started it. They're always causing problems."

The hell they were. Those boys were respectful and always followed the rules. They knew better than to get into trouble because their mom wouldn't stand for that kind of behavior.

"Really. Are you sure about that? Because we all know you can't keep your mouth shut about anything. Like mother, like son. Always flapping his mouth when he shouldn't. I'm here to tell you if he keeps it up, you're going to keep seeing me until it stops. I'm going to shout it everywhere how rude and disrespectful you and your son are." Serenity smiled a pleasant smile as if they were having a lovely afternoon tea chatting about the nice weather. "We all know how you hate gossip if it's geared at yourself. Such a hypocrite."

"Get out of my salon. Now! I won't stand for this."

"Sure. I have better things to do with my time than to deal with a snotty two-faced woman like you." Serenity looked at Violet, who sat in a chair waiting for the commotion to end and for Sharon to get back to working on her hair. "I don't know why you get your hair done here, Violet. She always cuts your hair uneven, and you deserve better than that."

Sharon gasped, Violet looked away, and Serenity turned around, startled to see him, though it didn't stop her from moving forward and toward the exit. She grabbed his hand and exited first. Her foot caught on the vase sitting outside the door that had a picture of Santa flying with his eight reindeer on the side. Cam always thought the thing looked so gaudy because of the terrible painting of it. Santa looked like a red blob with poop flying his sleigh, not eight adorable reindeer. He also never understood what the purpose of the vase sitting outside was for. It didn't do anything but sit there. No flowers were inside it or anything.

It was a heavy piece. When her foot connected with it, she stumbled and would've fallen to the cold concrete if he hadn't been holding her hand and catching her fall. Nothing would've saved the vase, though. It wobbled and teetered for a few seconds before crashing to the side, splintering into pieces.

"Whoops. Thanks for catching me."

He squeezed her hand. "Anytime." Then he tugged her around the vase and nodded at the pizza joint next door. "Let's get that pizza."

They barely spared a glance at the vase. He figured he should feel a little bad it broke, but they did the world a favor getting rid of the gaudiness. And Sharon had treated Serenity with disrespect, not acknowledging her son was a bully. Karma at its finest.

"You bitch! You broke that on purpose. I'm calling the police."

Cam froze at Sharon's harsh words. Serenity turned first, letting go of his hand.

"I tripped. You had it too close to the door. I should sue for whiplash. It hurt my neck nearly falling from it."

Serenity said it so smoothly and with such conviction, Cam believed her that she had hurt herself. He doubted it, but she sounded convincing. Even Sharon hesitated, but then pulled out her phone.

"You can't come here, get into my face, break my property, and think it's okay."

Serenity took two steps toward her, shoving another finger in her face, yet she didn't touch Sharon. "You can't pretend your son isn't a big bully, ignore his behavior, teach him how to treat people so rudely, talk shit about people behind their back, and think it's okay."

"How dare you," Sharon hissed with disbelief.

"No, how dare you!"

Sharon never got the chance to call the police. Cam suspected someone had when the police cruiser parked in the middle of the road, blocking traffic.

Officer Stephen Mahone stepped out of the car and approached the scene. Stephen made quick eye contact with him but said nothing. There were more important things to deal with, but Stephen hadn't spoken to him since Melanie cheated on him with his former best friend. Stephen had picked a side, and it hadn't been his.

Chaos ensued. Sharon started screaming about Serenity and her destruction of property, demanding her arrest. Serenity spat back about Sharon's behavior and how she felt unsafe in her presence and demanded her arrest in return. Cam stood silently by Serenity's side, praying this didn't escalate into any handcuffs being pulled out. He might not speak to Stephen anymore, but it didn't mean he wouldn't step in if he had to. He'd throw a punch if it came down to it. He'd secretly enjoy it too. He would've never imagined in a million years that one of his friends would steal his longtime girlfriend right from under his nose. He never would've thought another one of his friends would take the cheating friend's side. That hurt almost worse. Insinuating he was the bad guy for some reason. Like he was the one who had done something wrong.

"You could do so much better than this two-bit whore, Cam. She'll cheat on you like she did on her ex! You deserve better after Melanie hurt you," Sharon declared, suddenly changing her direction of the fight.

He flinched. Serenity tensed.

The entire sidewalk went silent.

Because they were friends.

Sharon just made it into something more.

For that, he'd never forgive her. He had wanted to announce his intentions on his own terms, not have someone else throwing it into Serenity's face.

"And you deny your son is a bully. All anyone needs to do is hear how you speak to know where he gets it from." Serenity looked at Stephen. "Add harassment charges while you're at it."

The arguing started back up as if it never stopped.

Cam didn't know whether to laugh, cry, or scream to stop it all. So he stood quietly, waiting for Stephen to step in and do something—anything.

Well, besides pulling out his handcuffs and slapping them on Serenity. Which he did to Cam's horror. Before Sharon could finish the triumphant smile spreading across her lips, he grabbed Sharon's right hand and put the other cuff on her wrist.

"There. That's settled. Now who wants to speak?" Stephen asked, darting his attention between the two women.

There was silence once more. Cam wanted to holler for him to get that thing off Serenity, yet he knew Stephen was teetering on the edge of hauling both of them to the station.

"I do not want to be handcuffed to this woman," Sharon sneered.

Stephen shrugged. "I only have one pair on me. You both kept screaming at me to arrest the other one. I know how to listen to women."

Cam barely suppressed a snort at that.

Serenity released a deep breath. "I want her son to leave my sons alone. To not be a big bully. I imagine he's not just picking on my boys."

Stephen nodded. "I have heard the same thing."

Sharon gasped. Then she looked contrite, dropping her gaze to the ground. "I'll speak to my son about his behavior. But I do not want this woman near my salon again."

"It's a public area outside, but I'm sure Serenity understands you don't want her entering your establishment." Stephen looked at Serenity for confirmation she heard him. Her tight nod said she had.

"Well, then. That wasn't so hard."

Stephen proceeded to unlock the handcuffs, and both women took several steps away from each other as soon as they were free.

"Am I free to leave?" Serenity asked with controlled patience.

The moment Stephen nodded, she turned around, grabbed his hand, and stalked away.

The warmth from the pizza joint might've given him a jolt to the system after standing outside so long in the freezing cold, but it did nothing to soothe his nerves. Serenity was shaking herself.

"Hey, you did great out there." Cam thought about wrapping his arm around her shoulder and pulling her closer but stopped himself. The last thing he needed was more talk around town about them. After Sharon screamed about it on the sidewalk, there would definitely be talk.

And he wasn't so sure about anything anymore. Sharon's accusation Serenity had cheated on her ex had him wondering. Had she? He'd never heard that before. The last thing he needed was to fall for another woman who'd do that to him again. He had never thought Melanie would rip his heart out like that. What a fool he'd been. He'd rather not fall into that trap again.

"I wanted to punch her dumb face and then stomp all over the broken pieces of that ugly vase."

Cam chuckled, and she looked at him at the sound. "It was ugly. You did the world a favor."

The deep frown she had been wearing morphed into a gentle grin. "I'm so glad you came. Thank you."

"Like I said, anytime."

As much as he hated ignoring the weird tension he could feel between them since Sharon's outburst, he would. For now. But they'd have to have a conversation later about it.

To break the tension.

For his sanity.

He wanted her, but he needed to know the truth. Would she hurt him like Melanie had?

3
———————

As soon as they stepped inside the house and closed the door, the boys were rushing into the living room. Serenity didn't even try to stop them from taking the pizza boxes from her.

"Wash your hands before you eat," she reminded them as they scrambled out of the room.

Her eyes glided to Cam when he chuckled. She shared in the moment with him, her heart beating a little wilder than it should be. She had an entire car ride by herself to calm down from everything that happened. It didn't help to erase the tension that had been created by Sharon's outburst.

What a bitch! Claiming she cheated on Eric. She'd tried everything in her power to make their relationship work, and he was the one who kept failing on his part. Working long hours, leaving her home alone with twin babies. Making excuses why he couldn't make holidays and special events. If anything, she had worried he was cheating on *her*. She never did find proof, only suspicion. He had definitely cheated on her with his work. That's all he ever talked about when they were together. Work, work, work.

They removed their shoes in silence. She took his coat and hung it up in the closet before heading to the dining room where the boys had already grabbed plates and napkins and were digging into the pizza.

"Why are there onions on this half of the pizza?" Royce asked with a disgusted grimace. He hated onions and most vegetables. Of course, what kid liked vegetables, she always reminded herself when the boys put up a fuss about eating them. She didn't argue about onions, but she put her foot down when it came to anything green.

"I like them." Cam winked as he took a seat on the other side of the table from her. "But I know you don't. That's why I only asked for it on half of it."

"Yeah, okay, makes sense." Royce grabbed two pieces of pepperoni and put them on his plate. "You wanna play some video games when we're done?"

Cam nodded. "Love to."

Serenity liked how her boys didn't even question why Cam was there. They were so used to him hanging around, it was normal. That's why it made her sad when Eric came around every so often and the awkwardness was there. The boys didn't know how to act around their father because he was so absent. At least they had a good man around who was a decent role model. Someone had to do it, since their father couldn't be bothered to do so.

They ate, chatting about the video game they'd be playing soon, and had a wonderful supper. She wanted to have a pleasant meal before she brought the mood down. Honesty with her boys was always an important part of the relationship they had. She tried to foster communication and trust with them. Without it, she thought things would falter and fall apart. As a single mom, she needed to trust her boys. She wasn't always around, working some nights at the diner. She was lucky enough to work from home during the day. Sometimes even getting housework done in between working on reports for the accounting company she worked for.

"So I made a phone call to the bus company and emailed the school about what happened today."

Randall didn't say anything. The only way he acknowledged he heard her was to lower his gaze to the empty plate before him. Royce didn't say anything either.

"I also had a chat with Sharon, Dawson's mother. He shouldn't be bothering you anymore, but if he does, I want to know."

"It's not a big deal," Randall muttered under his breath.

"It is a big deal. No one should treat you like that."

"Thanks, Mom," Royce said with a half-grin. "Isn't she like the biggest gossip in town?"

The fact that even her boys knew that about her said enough.

"Yes, she is."

"You just made it worse," Randall mumbled, his eyes still not leaving his plate.

Well, she hoped not, and it hadn't gone how she'd planned. Right from the start, when she approached Sharon about what happened, Sharon had gone on the defensive. Claiming her boy had done nothing wrong. It made her anger boil even more. Denying what was right in front of her eyes, though she shouldn't be surprised. He learned it from his mother.

"No one makes fun of my boys and gets away with it. I will always protect you, Randall, even if you don't agree with it."

Randall pushed away from the table and stalked out of the room. Royce stood up and paused. "Maybe we'll play games another night, Cam?"

Cam nodded. "Anytime, bud."

Then Royce left the room.

"Was I wrong?"

She hated that she doubted herself. Parenting was the hardest job she'd ever had. Every day she worried she was doing it all wrong. Second-guessing every decision she made. Wondering if she should've done it differently and if she had, if the outcome would've been the same or different —worse.

"No, you did what you thought was right."

Hmm. Suggesting he would've done something differently? How could she have done anything differently? She couldn't let it slide. Let that boy keep picking on Randall. If the school and bus company wouldn't do anything about it, then it was her job to do so.

"Hopefully, this solves the issue. Sharon will talk to Dawson and he'll stop." Cam put his napkin on his plate. "Unfortunately, bullying doesn't stop when you turn into an adult. That's something the boys will learn too."

That was such a true statement. Perhaps she handled the situation all wrong. Getting into Sharon's face like she had. Making a scene. Her boys would no doubt hear about it, and what kind of example was she setting? Not a very good one. Because that's not how she wanted them to solve issues when they got older. She had to do better. Next time —there better not be a next time—she'd do better. She would still approach Sharon, but privately. Not make a scene. Try to have an adult conversation with her, not fight like they were going to war.

"I didn't trip on the vase," she quietly confessed.

Cam's lips curled into a delicious smile. "It'll be our little secret. Seriously, you did the world a favor there."

She giggled, so thankful he showed up and stuck around. Even with all the chaos of the night. She stood, grabbing her plates and the boys' that they should've put in the kitchen themselves. Cam followed her with the rest of the stuff from the table. He threw away the pizza boxes in the garage after putting the few slices left in a container and in the fridge. She started loading the dishwasher. Normally, the boys took care of the dishes at night, taking turns, but tonight, she'd let it slide. Lots of emotions running high, and they deserved one night off to let them settle at their own pace.

"Do you want a drink before you go?" she asked when he came back inside, finishing putting the last two plates in the appliance.

"Sure." Cam grabbed two beers from the fridge, opened them, and handed her one once she finished.

They made their way to the living room, sitting next to each other on the couch. It was something they always did. She always tried to ignore that he sat so close, that his body heat set her own alive with too many sensations she had missed.

Tonight, it was hard to do so.

There was space between them. Enough where she could put her hand on the couch and not touch his thigh, but there wasn't enough to erase the sexual tension swirling through the air.

She didn't feel like watching TV, and she suspected neither did Cam. They had to clear the air, even if it would be a difficult conversation. Damn Sharon for even creating this awkwardness between them.

"So about—"

"We should—"

They laughed, then they both took a sip of beer and stared at each other. Were they on the same page about the conversation? She was going to say something about Sharon. He started to say they should—what? Talk about it? Should go out? Should forget it ever happened? Silence still filled the room.

"Sharon shouldn't have said what she did." She almost blew out a breath that Cam decided to speak first. "I'm sorry if the town thinks we're an item now."

Sorry?

As in, he wasn't interested?

Her heart deflated, even though she had told herself she wouldn't date him. Now he was taking the option off the table. It wasn't even a possibility.

Well, good. No need for her to worry about losing one of her good friends. It was nice to have a guy friend she could count on. To talk to about anything. To get advice about how to handle the boys when it came to delicate matters that their father should be handling.

She shrugged and chuckled. "It's no big deal. They know better. We've never given the impression we wanted more with each other."

Thank goodness she hadn't. How embarrassing would it have been if she put herself out there and he turned her down. Her sister read him wrong. He didn't have a thing for her.

He nodded with a weak smile. "Yeah, of course, we haven't. I like our friendship."

"Exactly. Why ruin a good thing?"

"Yep. My thoughts too." He kept nodding, then took a sip of beer.

"So we're good? No weirdness from what she said."

"No, no weirdness." He smiled to confirm it, yet she felt like he was forcing it.

But she couldn't blame him. She was dragging out a smile against her will as well. So much for there not being any weirdness left. If anything, the tension had increased.

"You called me and left a message. Something about a surprise."

He looked startled, as if he hadn't meant to leave that message, then the expression vanished as if it never existed. "Yeah, it's nothing big."

"Well, silly," she said with another fake smile and laugh, then slapped his thigh lightly in a jest, "what is it?"

He froze for a moment, then shifted on the couch. She swore it was a few inches more toward the other end. Away from her. Okay, message received loud and clear. She wouldn't touch him again.

"Umm...my brother has extra tickets to the *Nutcracker* showing tomorrow night. I thought you and the boys might like it. I know how much you like Christmas...and stuff."

She *hated* the *Nutcracker*. While they had watched it this summer, she hadn't enjoyed one moment of it. Royce had insisted, since a girl he liked in summer camp was talking about it and he wanted to impress her. Of course, she couldn't let anyone know she hated the play. Heaven forbid her boys found out she despised the holiday. That would suck all the joy out of it for them. She would never do anything to ruin the fun for her boys. Because once they knew she didn't like something, they made it their life's mission to never do it again. Her boys took care of her in more ways than she could count. She was blessed to have such wonderful children. Eric had no idea what he was missing. Loser.

Was she too enthusiastic about Christmas? Obviously, if

Cam thought she adored everything about the dumb holiday. She hadn't meant to overplay her fake love for it. She simply didn't want everyone to know how much she despised it, then be forced to talk about why she didn't like it. Talking about it was painful. Even thinking short thoughts hurt her deep inside. Like right now. She could feel the pain enveloping her heart, crushing her.

"That's so nice of you. But the boys have a sleepover planned with a friend. They can't go."

Cam's expression fell, not that he was super enthused to begin with. The night had turned very stilted the moment they chatted about Sharon.

"Well, I mean, you and I can still go. If you want. As friends, of course. Because that's what we are. Friends." Then a bright smile spread across his face.

Of course. She knew that. He didn't have to remind her over and over. She knew he only meant as friends. He made that abundantly clear a few minutes ago.

But she didn't want to endure a whole two hours or whatever it would be of the *Nutcracker*. She despised that play. It was nauseatingly boring.

The hopeful twinkle in his eyes—unless her own eyes were deceiving her—said she shouldn't say no. That, even though the boys wouldn't be around, she had to keep the ruse up that she loved Christmas. She didn't want it getting around town she hated the holiday. Then her boys would find out and they'd be crushed. Not that she thought Cam would spread gossip about her.

"Yeah, okay. We can do that. I work at the diner early Saturday instead of the evening, so I can't stay out too late."

Ugh. She didn't have to be a bitch about it. Not that she was lying about working the next day. She had picked up an extra shift to help out Tara, who had lost another waitress two weeks ago. They were stretched thin until she found another person to fill the position. She had to be there at six a.m. Gross. She loved sleeping in, and the weekends were the only opportunity she got to do so.

"To the play and back."

"Sounds good. It's a...night out."

He nodded again in that weird way he had done before with an awkward grin back on his face.

Yeah, she understood it this time.

Because she had almost said, "It's a date." But it wasn't, and saying it was would only increase the awkwardness levels to disastrous.

Oh, dear. She went to confront Sharon tonight to make her boys' lives easier, and it only made hers harder.

"Bro, I need two tickets to the *Nutcracker* tonight."

Cam pulled the phone away from his ear when Vin hooted with laughter. It wasn't funny. He needed these tickets or he would die of embarrassment. To tell Serenity he had the tickets and then having to tell her he actually didn't would not go over well. She hadn't seemed too enthused about going, but he chalked that up to the friends talk. He had no idea how that went sideways either, so he tried not to think about it. Of course, his dumb brain did anyway. All last night as he tried to sleep. All through the shower when he got up, hoping and praying his brother could pull through for him today. All through his morning coffee that tasted like mud instead of the golden liquid he usually created.

"Dude, you're insane. That show has been sold out for the past three weeks. It's not happening."

That wasn't what he wanted to hear.

"I need them."

"Why? I mean, it's not going to change the outcome, but why?"

Cam groaned, rubbing a tired hand down his face. Dealing with his younger brother could be exhausting, but it had more to do with the fact he had trouble sleeping last night.

"I told Serenity I had tickets to it and she agreed to go with me. I need two tickets. Come on, Vin. I don't ask a lot from you. Work a miracle here."

"What, that massive sleigh didn't do the trick and impress her? Grow some balls and tell her how you feel."

He did *not* need dating advice from a serial dater. Vin slept with as many women as he could, and Cam tried not to think about it. It was disgusting. He dated his high school sweetheart all four years in high school and all through college, until she cheated about a year after they graduated. After her, he was much more selective about dating. He didn't avoid women at all costs, but he also didn't put himself out there a lot. He didn't sleep with a woman just to have sex. It had to mean something for him. Not like Vin, who saw a set of boobs that impressed him and say no more. The woman made it to his bed, end of story.

"I haven't given her the sleigh yet."

And he wasn't even sure he should. She made it clear she only wanted to be friends. Why ruin a good thing? She was right. Why should they?

Oh, only for the reason he loved her and wanted to see if they could work. It might be worth trying to ruin it. Well, not ruin it, improve it. Take their friendship to another level. What was so wrong with that?

The only thing that would make it wrong was if she had

cheated on her ex. If she had, she'd do the same to him. He was a firm believer in once a cheater, always a cheater. He hadn't found his courage last night to ask her outright about it. Maybe he would tonight. Find a good way to insert it into their conversation. Make it seem like it wasn't a big deal—when it was a huge deal. Massive. Like a make-or-break deal for him.

But he could only do that if his brother pulled through for him.

"Please, Vin."

"Why would you invite her to a play you don't even have tickets for? It's sold out!"

It popped out without thinking about it. She mentioned the voicemail he left about a surprise he had for her. Which had been the sleigh, and he made a split-second decision he couldn't take back. He wasn't ready to give her the sleigh. But a play would work. Something he had tried to include the boys in too. So it wouldn't seem like a date.

And she made that quite clear last night it wasn't a date.

"I don't know. I just did. I need the tickets. Help me out here."

Vin sighed. "Let me see what I can do. Don't hold your breath, bro. It's a sold-out show."

He hung up with Vin, his nerves jumping like the peppiest, craziest Christmas song there was. If his brother failed him, he'd never be able to see Serenity again. The embarrassment would be too much.

Four hours later, while working on a bathroom cabinet, Vin came through for him like a little brother should. Two tickets to the *Nutcracker*. Not the best seats in the house, but beggars couldn't be choosers. He would've even taken ones with the view obstructed. Anything to make him not a liar.

He texted Serenity about what time he'd pick her up,

skipping mentioning having dinner first. It wasn't a date. He wouldn't treat it like one. She made no mention about it either. Though he knew it shouldn't have bothered him, it pierced him through the heart like a swift sword shoving deep inside.

Confirmed: not a date.

He picked her up on time, wanting to compliment her on how beautiful she looked, but figuring that would make things awkward. Like last night had been. He'd liked her since the first time he met her. Hell, even before that. The first time he had seen her at the snowman contest, he'd fallen head over heels. He'd wanted to know every little thing about her.

From the very beginning, despite his secret feelings, nothing had ever been uncomfortable between them. Not until last night.

Thanks a lot, Sharon.

They made it to the theater with minimal traffic, which was surprising since the play was several towns away. A Friday night on a busy highway he anticipated more traffic than they had, which put them to the theater earlier than he expected. No problem. They ordered a drink and walked around the venue to pass some of the time.

They checked their coats at the door. The red dress that fit her curves with delight had his heart pumping and his cock begging to be released. Thinking different measurements in his head helped to keep it at bay and not noticeable. Though it also made it hard to focus on the conversation while reciting this length of board to that length of board in his head.

"You look lovely tonight." There. He said it. Because he had to. He couldn't *not* say it. Her beauty damn near took his breath away.

Her shoulders were bare, yet it wasn't a revealing dress in the front or back. It was classy with a touch of sassiness to it. Maybe because it was red and he always attributed red with sexy. It went past her knees, though he could still see her calves. The red stilettos she wore finished it out with finesse. His mind kept veering toward inappropriate thoughts about the heels alone. Nothing but that on her as he took her deep, pounding into—

"Thank you. I had to borrow it from my sister. I almost couldn't get it zipped."

She interrupted his thoughts, but that only wanted to pull him back into them with ease. Especially when his eyes glided up and down the length of her trying to figure out what the hell she was talking about. The dress fit her like a glove. It didn't look too tight. It looked perfect, extenuating her curves with delicious delight.

"Red suits you. I like it."

Her smile widened, then disappeared behind her wine glass as she took a sip. "You look rather dashing yourself." She reached out and swiped at his shoulder as if adjusting the lapel to his jacket. "I like you in a suit."

He shivered, not from the cool temps in the theater. He figured the heat was on, but all he'd been feeling since they arrived was coolness surrounding him. It was an old building, so it didn't have the best ventilation system. Serenity didn't appear to be cold. He hadn't seen her shiver once, and he figured he would've since she didn't have a shawl or anything to put over her bare shoulders.

But oh, no, he shivered from her light touch. Something she rarely did. Yet, in the past two days, once last night and just now, she'd touched him. On the thigh that had him aching to reach forward and pull her closer. Kiss her until she begged for a moment of air. Now on his shoulder. That shouldn't feel sexual, but it only made him ache to reach for her and touch her in return. Twirl the loose strand hanging by her cheek around his finger. Glide his hand across her cheek in a soft caress. Slide his hand behind her back and pull her firmly to his side. Anything just to touch her. Give her a small sign that he wanted more than friends. Much, much more.

"I only have it for occasions like this. I don't dress up much."

Wow. Dumb. He should stop talking. Way to impress a woman by admitting he rarely dressed up. He made himself sound like a slob or something.

She took another sip of her drink. He followed suit because he didn't know what else to say or do. She smacked her lips a few times, rubbing them together as if making sure her lipstick was spread evenly on her lips. He shifted his feet.

The uneasiness between them spread like wildfire.

"It's still—"

"Why does—"

Laughter filled the air. Talking at the same time again.

Last night he spoke first, clarifying his broken sentence, and he felt like he said it all wrong. He'd let her go first this time. It's still, what? Weird between them? Definitely.

"I hate this..." She motioned her hand between them, shaking her head as if trying to find the right words.

She hated...what? Him? Them? Being friends? Maybe he should've spoken first. If he lost her completely from his life, he didn't know how he'd survive it. Being friends was better than nothing. And he'd miss hanging out with Royce and Randall too. They reminded him so much of him and Vin growing up. Sure, they weren't twins like Royce and Randall, but they only had two years between them, and they did everything together. Stuck up for each other when kids tried to pick on one or the other. Covered for each other when their parents found out something they shouldn't have. They were as close as two brothers could be. Even if Vin did annoy him sometimes.

"I hate the awkwardness between us. Why is it still there?"

The knife that had pricked his heart when he thought she might hate him dissolved and disappeared.

"I don't know."

Sure you do, idiot! Because you love her and she doesn't love you back. She only wants to be friends.

"I don't want it to be there, Cam."

"Me either." Far from it. And if he confessed his feelings now, it would only increase.

"Oh, God, hide me." She grabbed his arm and wrapped hers around it, shocking him to the core.

Damn if his cock didn't spring for joy she was touching him once again. And still touching him. Leaning into him so much, he wanted to find an empty room and show her how much he loved her sweet hands on him.

"Eric, what a surprise to see you here. I didn't realize you liked plays," Serenity said with no pleasantry whatsoever.

Cam drew his attention to the sharp-dressed man in front of them. He'd materialized out of nowhere. Obviously not, since Serenity had spied him first and clung to him like a crab to a net.

The boys' father.

The deadbeat dad that didn't care.

Cam wasn't around all the time, but he was around enough to know they didn't see their father often. Serenity didn't talk about him much, not even when the boys weren't around. She never said anything when they were in listening distance. He knew based on the little she had said that she didn't like Eric. Or more like she didn't appreciate his lack of attention with the boys.

"I didn't realize you liked the *Nutcracker*," he replied smoothly as if pretending he didn't hear the derision in her tone.

He had black hair slicked back into a greasy doo that said he spent too much time getting it to look just right. His suit fit him to perfection, and his bright-white teeth annoyed Cam for some reason. As if he spent too much money to get the perfect teeth when he could've been spending that money on his sons.

"You didn't return my call. About Christmas."

Cam felt awkward—yet again—being near a conversation that he shouldn't be listening to. But Serenity was still clinging to his arm, and he wasn't about to shove her away. Why was she clinging to his arm?

Whatever. He didn't care. He'd soak up this moment because he'd never get it again. Not with the way his luck was going.

"Yeah, I've been busy. I was going to."

"And?"

Cam couldn't see her face clearly, but he felt her roll her eyes.

"And I'm not sure I can take them next weekend. I have a big thing with work and it's going to be tough."

"You haven't seen them in three months. That's all you have to say."

"Work keeps me busy. I don't know what you want me to say."

Serenity inhaled deeply before letting it out through her teeth. "Do you plan on seeing them at all for Christmas?"

"Yeah, sure, I'll look at my calendar. I should be able to

make something work." Eric turned his gaze at him. "Who's this?"

"He's someone who acts like a father to the boys more than you do."

Cam tensed. Eric looked pissed. Serenity clung to him tighter.

"Just because you're sleeping with her doesn't make my boys yours," Eric said, his lips thin and his eyes blazing with murder.

Serenity placed a hand on his chest, which was a good thing because he felt rage bubbling to the surface. Eric didn't care about his boys. And if he did, he had a terrible way of showing it. Honestly, it was her fault. She did not have to say what she did. Even if it was true. There was no need to hold him back. No matter how much he was tempted to throw a punch at this jerk, he never would. Violence wasn't the answer in his eyes. But maybe she had done it for show. Make Eric think he'd retaliate with more than just words.

Or she placed her hand there to tell him to keep quiet. When she spoke, he interpreted it that way. "He shows up when he says he will. That's more than you ever do, Eric. Figure out your work shit and take the boys next weekend like you said you would how many months ago. Now, if you'll excuse us, we have to find our seats. I expect to hear from you on Monday."

Then Serenity pulled him to follow her and he did. It would look stupid if he kept standing there saying nothing. What was wrong with him? He should've spoken up, even if she had started it. Though the hand to his chest was answer enough. She hadn't wanted him to say anything.

Instead of heading into the theater, she pulled them toward a quiet corner and finally let go of his arm. He didn't see the drink in her hand and wondered when she set it down. He could tell by the way she twisted her hands, she wished she hadn't ditched it. Her nervous energy was too much.

"I'm so sorry, Cam. I don't know why I said that. Or why I did that. Eric..." She gritted her teeth and seethed quietly, suppressing a scream. "I hate him so much sometimes."

"Did you cheat on him?"

What the hell was wrong with him? Did that really come out of his mouth? She hated him so much she cheated on him? He took it out on the boys instead of her?

By her crestfallen expression, he wished he could take it back.

4

THIS WAS *NOT* a conversation she wanted to have. Especially
with Cam. Despite talking about the weirdness last night, it
was still simmering and swirling around them. Telling him
about her relationship with Eric wouldn't make it any better.
She hated talking—let alone thinking—about Eric.

Cam shook his head, his cheeks burning bright red. "I'm
sorry. I shouldn't have asked that. It's none of my business."

Serenity ached to touch him again. Reach out and curl
her arm around his, making it that much easier to wrap her
body against his. She knew he had a toned body. It wasn't
hard to see the thick muscles lining up and down his arms,
the sculpted chest that made his T-shirts look too tiny on
him. She drooled at the sight this past summer when he
took his shirt off and the sweat glistened on his chest and
back while cutting down a dead tree in her yard.

Those brief moments she clung to him a short minute
ago had been heaven. Had been too much of a temptation,
and that's why she couldn't touch him again. Her resolve
might crumble, and that couldn't happen.

"Do you think I cheated on him?"

After shouting and arguing with her mind and body not to move a muscle and fling herself at him, his question hit her square in the heart.

Why would he ask her such a thing? He only would if he thought she'd do something so callous to another person.

His brows were low, his eyes filled with pain, his shoulders slumped as if he were admitting defeat. To what? For what reason?

"No, I don't. I can't picture it at all." His mouth fell into an even grimmer stance. "But I also didn't think my girlfriend of eight years—all through high school and college— would cheat on me either. With my best friend. I guess you could say I don't trust my instincts anymore."

She'd heard rumors about his ex-high school sweetheart, though had never heard the words directly from his mouth—until now. How heartbreaking for him. She tried not to take it personally that he'd ask her such a question, but in the same token, she understood why he would.

Like a sudden burst of sunlight through a dreary cloud, Cam smiled. "Like I said, it's not my business and I shouldn't have asked. We're just friends."

Right. Just friends. The more she was reminded of it, the more she hated it.

"Let's find our seats." Then he gestured for her to take the lead, though didn't touch her on the back to guide her out of the tiny alcove they had found themselves in.

She was grateful and crushed at the same time.

Her own bright smile appeared as she led the way. Cam finished his drink and set it down on a side table before they entered the theater. Their seats were on the mezzanine level. Though they were far away from the stage, it didn't bother her. Halfway through the play, she dozed off.

A light jostling startled her, making her sit upright in

her seat. She turned to Cam who had a goofy grin on his face.

"You fell asleep," he whispered. Of course, the people around them were filing out of their seats indicating the show was over. He didn't need to speak quietly because the noise in the theater was loud enough to drown out whatever they said.

How embarrassing. She'd never fallen asleep at a show before. Movie or play. What a dead giveaway she had no interest whatsoever in the *Nutcracker*. Thank goodness the boys hadn't come with.

"It's been a long week. I guess I didn't realize how tired I was. I'm so sorry."

He shrugged, the mellow grin still prominently displayed. "I understand. You're cute when you're sleeping. Your head bobbing up and down."

Laughter spilled out, the embarrassment intensifying. Of course, she was laughing with him, knowing how ridiculous she had looked.

"You should've woken me up!"

His smile wavered a fraction, and concern sprang forth in his gaze. "I know how hard you work, Serenity. I know you have to get up early tomorrow. I shouldn't have insisted you come with." Then his lips widened once again. "I didn't let your head bob for long. I let you rest it on my shoulder. You only drooled a little."

Her mouth dropped open in shock, wiping at her lips and chin as if saliva still lingered. Then she slapped his chest playfully when the glee in his eyes said he was joking with her.

"That's not funny."

"It was a little funny. You should've seen your face." Still chuckling, he stood up and reached out his hand. "Come on. Let's get you home and into bed."

Her body instantly pooled with desire. Yes, into bed. With him.

For the second time that night, his cheeks flamed a bright red. She loved that Cam could blush. This time not in a bad way or for the wrong reasons. Well, jumping into bed with him wouldn't be a wise decision. But it didn't make her stop wanting it with every breath in her body.

She slid her hand into his and allowed him to pull her to her feet. He didn't yank hard, yet she found herself chest to chest with him once she was level, her hand still tucked into his.

"Thank you for a nice night out, Cam."

"It was sort of bumpy. You sure it was that nice?"

His soft voice slid over her like a sweet caress. She wanted to move closer, wrap herself so tightly around him it'd take days for him to pry her away. Yet they were in a full theater, people surrounding them, and it would be so embarrassing to throw herself at a man who would only push her away. Friends only. They had agreed.

"Any time I spend with you is always nice. Some parts were unpleasant, but nothing's perfect in life. I'd rather have an iffy day with you than anyone else because you can still manage to turn it around and make me laugh."

They stood there, breathing heavier as the moment wore on. The noise died down as the theater emptied.

"Take me home, Cam."

He nodded and smiled, turning around, her hand still tucked inside his. They held hands the entire way out of the theater and to his car. It was the first time they had ever done so. Sure, she had grabbed his hand last night a few times, but that was to escape a scene. They generally didn't hold hands. She found she liked it. She'd never even held hands with Eric when they had been together. Of course, Eric had never been a PDA kind of guy. He was always about appearances and what people might think.

They made it to her house faster than she liked. The ride had been silent, although not in an awkward way. At least, not in a bad awkward way. There was still that underlying sexual tension floating between them.

He parked the truck and turned it off, opening his door first. Okay, so they were getting out right away. No small talk in the vehicle before he walked her to the door. Something he didn't have to do, but Cam was always a gentleman. Even if they had designated this as not a date, he'd still walk her to the door.

Would he kiss her?

Why would he? They had already established this wasn't a date.

Yet those last moments before they left had changed the dynamics between them. She'd felt it as if someone had sucker-punched her. She couldn't keep ignoring it.

She unlocked her door with steady hands when nothing she was about to do made her steady at all. She could feel her nerves jacking up to scary heights.

Before twisting the handle, she turned around. "Thanks for a lovely evening. Bumpy parts and all."

"Thanks for coming with me. I always enjoy myself with you."

They stared at each other. She bit her bottom lip, then smoothed it out with her tongue. He followed the movement, his eyes portraying what he wanted, yet he still hadn't made a move.

Was she going to have to make the first move?

"Do you want to have a drink before you leave?"

He didn't lift his wrist to check his watch. "It's after ten. You have to get up early. I don't want to be the cause you're dead tired on your feet tomorrow. Sleep well."

His body twisted to leave and she couldn't have that. If he rejected her outright when she made it clear what she wanted, then so be it. She'd live and move on like she always did. She'd ignore how much it would rip her heart out if he did so.

She grabbed his hand, halting his movement. He turned back her way.

"I want you to stay, Cam."

His jaw clenched hard. "I can't walk inside that house, Serenity."

A gust of wind slapped her in the face. Or was it his words? His rejection?

"Why not?"

A muscle in his cheek contracted, making him look more menacing than she'd ever seen him look. "We're friends. That's what we said."

"Sometimes friends...sleep with each other."

He swallowed hard. "Is that all it would be? Friends with benefits? Because once we cross that line, there's no coming back."

"We already crossed a line if we're even having this conversation. How do we come back from that? It's been weird between us since yesterday. I want the weirdness gone."

"And sleeping together will make it go away?"

She didn't know how to answer that. Probably because she knew as well as him that nothing would make it go away. She felt like they only had two options here: sleep together and find out, or never see each other again.

It was all that bitch's fault. Damn Sharon!

"I never cheated on Eric. I'm not that kind of woman. When I'm with someone, it's only them."

Cam nodded, frowning. "I know. I believe you. But I can't sleep with someone just for sex. I'm not that kind of guy. When I'm with someone, I want it to mean something."

She felt herself losing him, which was crazy because she was still holding his hand.

"What are you saying, Cam?"

"I'm saying, get a good night's rest. We'll pretend this conversation never happened. Let's not ruin a good thing." He leaned forward and brushed his lips against her cheek and then moved away, letting go of her hand. "Your friendship means more than you'll ever know. I don't want to lose that."

Wow. He didn't want to sleep with her. She'd read all the signals the wrong way. Before he could see the tears stream down her face, she turned toward the door and walked inside.

So much for putting herself out there. He rejected her. She honestly hadn't seen that coming.

"So, Hope wants to have a Christmas party. Not this weekend, but next. Family and friends. You'll be there."

Cam chuckled and looked up from the numbers he hadn't been seeing but trying to pay attention to. Ever since Saturday night when he left the woman he loved thinking he didn't want her, he'd been distracted.

Distracted with his idiocy.

Distracted with knowing he did the right thing.

Distracted with how he could make her realize how great they could be together. Not just in bed. As a couple.

"That sounded like I'm going whether I planned to or not."

Mase nodded. "You have to be there. Hope's going all out, and I need my best friend there. Always, man." Mase grinned. "You can invite Serenity to come with. Hope will if you don't, but it'll mean more coming from you."

"No, she'll think she wasn't wanted by Hope if Hope doesn't invite her."

Mase thought about it and then confirmed it with a tight nod. "You do have a point. You should still mention to her about driving together or something."

It'd been four days since he'd seen Serenity. Even talked to her. They had a habit of texting each other throughout the day, but since that disastrous night...nothing. Radio silence.

He feared he wouldn't be able to crawl himself out of the hole he'd created.

Of course, he could text her first, instead of waiting for her to reach out. But he figured if she wanted to talk to him, she'd let him know.

"I don't think so."

"Come on. Are you going to give up that easily?"

Cam had told Mase everything that happened. From Sharon causing a scene to meeting Eric to Serenity offering sex—with nothing attached to it. He wished he could be more like his brother Vin. Sleep with a woman and move on. Pretend it didn't mean anything other than extreme pleasure. Except he couldn't. The fact he loved Serenity only made it harder.

"No, but it's best we don't drive together. I'll have to drop her off again and..." His mind flickered to what happened the last time he'd dropped her off. Pure perfection had been his for the taking, and he walked away like it didn't matter. "And...and...I can't do it again."

Mase looked at the large sleigh still hiding in his workshop. They didn't have an official office for their business. Clients either found them word of mouth via a flyer they had hanging around the surrounding towns, or their website. Sometimes, they took out an advertisement in the local newspapers in the surrounding towns. They did all their paperwork at Cam's place most of the time. Though Mase always doubled checked he did a thorough job. Sometimes, he messed up a number or two, and it was good to have a second pair of eyes look over his work. They were in the black and had been for a very long time. Business was good. Cam didn't even need to go over the numbers yet, but he'd needed something to distract his mind. It wasn't working. Especially with Mase getting on his case about Serenity.

"When are you going to give her the sleigh?"

Never.

Cam shrugged instead of saying what popped into his head.

"The snowman building contest is this weekend. Are you entering? I bet Serenity is."

Unless Eric played dad for the weekend. Then she wouldn't have the boys and she wouldn't enter.

"It hasn't even snowed. How can they have the contest without snow?"

"There's some in the forecast for Friday."

"That's cutting it close."

"Yeah, but fresh snow will be great."

Cam grinned. "Only if it's sticky. This sounds like a losing battle."

"Well, I guess we can secretly cheer that it fails, since it is Mayor Hafferty's thing. But it went over well with the town last year, and Hope will do it again next year when she's officially mayor. We'll be there because, as the new mayor-elect, she wants to support it."

That all made sense. Hope had won the mayoral spot last month, and starting in January, the position would officially transfer to her. The event had been a success last year. The only problem was the lack of snow.

"Hope suggested—to Mayor Hafferty's disgust—that they move it to the ski resort outside of Mason because they have fake snow already. Of course it's not part of Mulberry, so he didn't like the idea."

"He'd like it if someone else thought of it," Cam replied. They both knew how much Mayor Hafferty hated Hope. Not because she won the latest election either. He just did. He portrayed himself as a nice guy, but deep inside, he was nothing but a snake. Cam felt bad for Mase that he was inadvertently marrying into that family. Hope's sister Chasity was married to Mayor Hafferty's son, Stu. Great guy. Cam didn't know how he turned out so great with such a nasty father.

Mase checked the time on his phone. "I better get going. Hope will be home soon, and I told her I'm making my famous homemade pizza."

Cam's mind veered to the last time he had pizza. With Serenity.

He waved good-bye to Mase, taking his parting advice, and put the company books away. He wasn't getting anything productive done anyway. A quick look at his phone showed it was almost six o'clock. Knowing Serenity, she already cooked supper. It wouldn't make sense to reach out about bringing pizza over or something.

Offer an olive branch. A peace offering. A sign that he

didn't want to lose her from his life, even if he wouldn't sleep with her for sex only.

He was such an idiot. He should've never walked away. He should've never told her no.

Four days of no communication had been stupid as well. She probably thought he never wanted to talk to her again. She had put herself out there and he rejected her. Why in the hell would she reach out first? She wouldn't.

"Idiot!"

He picked up his phone and found her number. He had to fix his mistake. His finger hit dial before he could change his mind. This required actual talking, not texting. He needed her to hear the sincerity in his voice. How sorry he was.

She answered on the third ring. "Hi."

"Hey. I hope I'm not bothering you."

Talk about stilted. The tension oozed between them like a hot muggy night.

"Not at all. Folding some laundry while the boys finish up the dishes."

So he had been right. They already ate. Predictable. They got home around four, did their homework, and she was preparing supper and setting it on the table between five and five-thirty every evening. The boys did their chores, showers, and then played video games until it was time to go to bed and wake up to do the same thing over and over again.

"What's up?" she asked, her voice slightly shaking.

Good to know she was as nervous as him about this conversation. Not that he wanted her to be nervous. She hadn't done anything wrong but be honest with him. He couldn't fault her for that.

"I miss you."

What? That was *not* what he meant to say. Except it was the truth. He missed her. Four days wasn't long, but it felt like years had dragged by when he was used to talking/texting with her almost every day.

"I'm sorry—"

"I'm sorry—"

They chuckled together.

"Let me go first," Serenity said, her tone sounded lighter since she answered. "You have nothing to be sorry about. I'm the one who's sorry for making it awkward between us. It was a lovely evening. I missed you too."

He could feel his heart rate, which had accelerated the moment he hit dial, start to slow down.

"Don't apologize either. You didn't do anything wrong."

He hoped she believed that, but by the soft sigh he heard she didn't. Well, it was the truth. Neither of them did anything wrong. It was something that shouldn't have happened and all they needed to do was move on. Forget about it.

"Are you and the boys entering the snowman contest in Mulberry this weekend? If so, I thought I'd try to bribe my way onto your team. I want to win. And since you won last year, I figure my chances are good."

Her sweet laughter filtered through the phone. "What's the bribery? It has to be good."

Sex. Lots and lots of sex.

Well, he couldn't say that. His eyes glided to the sleigh that filled up half his workshop.

"An early Christmas present."

Silence greeted him. He swore he even heard a low groan.

"You don't have to get me anything, Cam."

"I already have it."

More silence.

"Serenity, did I say something wrong?"

"No, of course not. Umm...I shouldn't tease you about it. The boys are going to be with Eric this weekend. We chatted on Monday and he swore he'll be here Friday to get them. As long as he keeps his word, it'll be just me."

Cam couldn't decide if that was better or worse. No boys meant more temptation. Because if Serenity mentioned sex again, he wasn't sure he could say no. It had been difficult to deny her the first time.

Of course he hadn't lied. He wanted more than sex. He wanted it all with her, or at least see if they could make a relationship work. If they didn't try, how would they ever know?

"Okay, no Christmas present." Yet, he silently told himself. Eventually, he'd have to give her the sleigh because he made it for her. "Do you want some company after the boys leave?"

Because he knew it wouldn't be easy for her. The boys were with her all the time. Eric rarely did his fatherly duties. He imagined she'd be worrying like crazy about how the boys were doing, if they were happy, how their father was treating them. He knew he'd be worrying about it. Because their happiness and well-being meant everything to him, even if he wasn't their father—or even stepfather. Hell, he wasn't even a boyfriend and he cared about them.

Her breath hitched as if she were on the verge of tears, and he wanted to be right next to her in an instant. Wrap her up in his arms and take all her pain and worries away. Tell her everything would be all right, even if he had no idea how to make things right.

"I'd like that. I'm worried about how this weekend is

going to go. The boys are excited, but Eric always manages to ruin it."

"I'll bring a bottle of wine."

"Make it a bottle of scotch," she said with maniacal laughter. "I'm going to need something strong."

"You got it." He almost added 'that's what friends are for,' but managed to stop himself. No need to point out the dreaded friend relationship they had when he wanted much, much more.

"I'm glad you called, Cam. I needed to hear your voice."

Cam didn't know what to say to that. Because it killed him inside.

He feared, despite what he heard between the lines, that she'd still only want sex from him and nothing else.

Damn his resolve, he was going to give in. This weekend.

5

"MAKE sure you don't lose your phones. If you go somewhere, bring it with you." Serenity stood in front of her boys, aching to reach out and smooth a hand across their heads and down their cheeks like she used to do when they were little. They didn't like all the mushy gestures—as they put it—that much anymore. Especially in public. They weren't in public. They stood in front of the door waiting for Eric to arrive. The bastard better not be late.

"If you need me, you call. I don't care what it's about."

It'd been three months since Eric had them for the weekend. The last time he picked them up, instead of keeping them until Sunday, he dropped them off on Saturday claiming a work thing came up he couldn't dismiss. Ha! Work thing? Yeah, right. She knew he just couldn't take the responsibility of raising two boys. Or any kids for that matter. He'd never been the lovey-dovey kind of father. Barely held them when they were babies. Didn't change one damn diaper. He might've helped create them, but he wasn't anywhere near close to being a father.

"Mom, we'll be fine. I promise. Dad said he's taking us to

an arcade tonight. It's gonna be epic," Royce said with more enthusiasm than she anticipated.

They didn't talk about their father much, and the rare times they did, they acted like they didn't care whether they saw him or not. As soon as she told them Monday night they'd be spending the weekend with Eric, their excitement had been through the roof.

Well, Royce's had. Randall, who stood there quiet and not looking at her, hadn't appeared thrilled at all.

"When did you talk to your dad?"

Because that was news to her. Not that they had to tell her every time they spoke to him. He had their number and vice versa. She'd finally caved in two years ago and got both of them a phone. One, because she liked knowing they didn't have to rely on Eric if they wanted to call her. Two, because they were involved in a lot of sports throughout the year. If they needed her before practice ended, she wanted them to be able to reach her without an issue.

"Yesterday," Royce answered a bit hesitantly as if he wasn't sure he should say anything.

She wasn't mad about it. She'd never be mad about it. Eric might not be the world's best dad, but that didn't mean she didn't want him to try. She wanted him to be more active in the boys' lives. She wanted him to care more about them than his dumb job.

"Well, that sounds like fun. You both have a wonderful time."

When Randall still wouldn't look at her, she gave in to her urge and reached out, rubbing her hand behind his head and to his cheek. He didn't shake her off or look at her, but she could hear the small sigh that released.

"I love you both. You're going to have fun. You know how I know? Because you're together and you always have fun together." Of course, she meant Royce and Randall, not Eric, but she didn't exclude Eric verbally because she never wanted to paint him as the bad guy. He did that so well all on his own.

"When's Cam coming over again?" Randall suddenly asked, finally looking at her.

Her hand fell to her side, surprised by the question. Sure, the boys were used to Cam coming around, but neither of them had ever asked for him like that. It most likely had to do with the fact they hadn't seen him in more than a week. It'd been radio silence from him until he called earlier in the week, not something she had shared with the boys. Usually, they saw Cam at least once or twice a week. Dropping by to say hello, bringing pizza, or helping to fix something in the house. Sometimes, she even purposely found something that needed fixing so she had a reason to call him. How pathetic was that!

"We still need to play those video games," Randall added.

"Well, I'm sure we can call him next week to come over for that."

Randall finally produced a short grin, nodding. "Don't forget to call him, Mom. He has to come over."

"I won't." She chuckled, curious about Randall's sudden insistence Cam come over. No need to tell them Cam was coming over tonight. She didn't want to explain why and make them think Cam was anything more than a friend.

Yet the way Randall asked about him and insisted he come over made her think Randall thought Cam was more than simply a friend. That wasn't good.

Was it?

She'd never had a serious boyfriend before. When she did date, bringing home a man to meet her boys was never on top of her to-do list. Her boys were her life and they would always come first. Always. No man would enter into their lives just because she was dating him. She never dated anyone long enough to *want* them to meet her boys.

Cam was always around. He fit in their little world as if he'd been meant to be there from the beginning.

A knock on the door startled her, causing the boys to laugh at her for jumping. Royce opened the door, his face beaming with happiness.

"Hey, Dad. You're early."

Serenity wanted to snort in derision at Royce's words but kept it in. One minute before the expected time wasn't that early. But whatever, she'd let her son have his excitement. She prayed Eric didn't do anything to ruin it. For him, being one minute early was pretty decent. Normally, he was twenty minutes or so late.

"Excited for this weekend, little man!" Eric said jovially as if he was. God, she hoped so. "Grab your bags and let's hit the road."

The boys hugged her, Randall a little more tightly than Royce, and then they grabbed their bags and headed outside.

"It's started to snow, so drive carefully."

Eric rolled his eyes. "I know how to drive in the snow. Thanks, Serenity."

She wasn't saying it to be an ass. He lived forty-five minutes away in a bigger town. He'd never liked the small-town atmosphere and left as soon as he could. While she hadn't been born and raised here, she fell in love as soon as she found this little diamond in the rough. That should've been clue enough when they bought this house that it was never going to work between them. He hadn't been thrilled about moving, and she had chalked it up to nerves at being a new father. They had decided living in a smaller town would be nice and a great place to raise the boys in. Apparently, he had lied about that idea, never sharing it with her as she had originally thought.

"Don't mess this up, Eric. They've been excited all week to see you."

"Your faith in me knows no bounds." Eric shook his head, then looked around the foyer. "Where's your boyfriend?"

If only Cam was her boyfriend.

He'd sleep with her then.

Ugh. She needed to get those thoughts right out of her head. He was coming over to soothe her rattled nerves with Eric taking the boys, not to have sex with her.

Because he was her friend. The best friend in the world.

"What time will you be dropping them off on Sunday again? By six, correct?"

She had no intention of indulging Eric's delusional jealousy. He hadn't cared about her in years, so she wasn't sure why he wanted to pretend now.

"Yeah, something like that. Have a nice weekend." His shit-eating grin said he didn't care if she did or not. He knew how hard this weekend would be for her being away from the boys for so long.

The door closed, shutting out the cold that had slipped past the defenses and taking her boys with it.

She had told Cam that Eric would be getting the boys around six, but he was always late, so to drop by around seven. The last thing she needed was Cam around when Eric was. Eric would ask more ridiculous questions that he had no business knowing anyway.

Of course, Eric had come early—only by a stupid minute—and now she had time to kill. No sense wasting good time. She put the laundry away she should've done last night. She swore she was doing at least a load a day. Those boys went through so many clothes, they had to be making multiple wardrobe changes a day.

The dishwasher wasn't finished with its cycle, so she couldn't put the clean dishes away. She thought about calling her sister, but she never had anything nice to say about Eric, and that would only increase Serenity's worries.

She fiddled with her phone so much, she was surprised she didn't drop it multiple times from the nerves she could feel swimming through her veins. All she wanted to do was text her boys and make sure they made it to Eric's safely. Or the arcade, if Eric kept his word. The snow wasn't coming down heavily, but it hadn't stopped since it started at three when school got out. If it kept it up, the plows would be working overtime. The roads could be bad in some spots.

But she wanted them to have their time with their father without her hovering. She couldn't constantly text them.

Ten minutes to seven, her phone chirped. The sharp noise startled her and she dropped her phone for the first time that night. Thankfully, she had a good protective case and not a scratch, dent, or crack appeared.

A wide smile split across her face. Her boys knew her so well.

> Randall: We made it to the arcade. It's a pretty cool place.
>
> Serenity: So glad to hear that. Have fun!
>
> Royce: We'll let you know when we get to dad's. Don't worry about anything mom.

How did she ever think she could fool them?

She sent a kissing emoji face and said she loved them to

the text thread and to have fun one more time. Her heart felt better already.

When the doorbell went off ten minutes later, her heart rate sped up.

Cam was here. On time. As usual.

She opened the door and it looked like a winter wonderland outside behind him. The snow was swirling in such erratic circles, she knew her anxiety would be through the roof until she received another text they made it to Eric's.

"That snow looks like a storm."

Cam looked over his shoulder, then back at her. He hesitated, then nodded. "It wasn't pleasant driving in it."

"Oh my gosh, Cam." She grabbed his arm and pulled him inside the warm house, shutting out the freezing cold one more time. "You should've called and turned around. I would never want you to get hurt driving in something like this."

"The wind started picking up about five minutes from your house. It wasn't that bad."

Her eyes narrowed into tiny slits. "Both of those statements contradict each other. It either wasn't pleasant or it wasn't that bad. It can't be both."

"It wasn't bad until about five minutes from your house when it became not pleasant." His warm smile did nothing to melt the icy terror running through her veins.

"They stopped at an arcade. Who knows how long they'll be there? It could get worse by the minute."

Cam's expression turned down, the worry plain as day in his eyes. He understood her worries.

"I'd say it was more on the good pleasant rather than a bad pleasant."

Sudden laughter slipped out, sounding more like a snort

from her. "Now you're not making sense and I thank you for it. This is why I needed you here. You can make anything seem not as terrible as it is. You make me laugh when I don't want to."

"I also brought the scotch," Cam said, lifting the bottle she hadn't noticed in his right hand.

"I'll get the glasses."

"And I'll pour them to the top."

———

THEY'D BEEN SITTING on the couch for the past hour talking about random stuff, sipping on their drinks, and ignoring the elephant in the room. The extreme sexual tension was off the charts. More so than the last time they'd been together.

Cam didn't want to keep ignoring it, but he also didn't want just sex. He wanted it all. He had no doubt that Serenity hadn't changed her mind about that.

"So, did you still sign up for the snowman building contest?" Cam asked, trying to think of more non-sexual things they could talk about. He was running out of ideas.

It was taking all his strength to stay on his side of the couch and not kiss her breathless. Her cheeks were a light shade of red, presumably from the scotch they were sipping. They were only on their second glass, and Cam didn't want to make it much more. If anything happened between them, he wanted it to be because they chose to, not because the alcohol said to do it.

Serenity shook her head and swiped a strand of hair behind her ear. "No, because Eric said he'd take the boys for the weekend. I only did it last year for them. And I wanted to think positive thoughts he'd actually do what he said this time." She swiped another hand behind her ear, no hair this time to pull out of the way. "Did you?"

"Umm, no. I didn't have high hopes the snow would come, and it's probably not going to be sticky enough to even make a snowman tomorrow. But I would've still bribed my way onto your team if you had signed up."

A smile lit up her face. "I need to know the bribe." Her eyes narrowed. "And not an early Christmas present."

How about a kiss?

Of course, he couldn't say that. And why did the Christmas present seem to bother her? For someone who loved Christmas, he figured she'd love to have an early present.

"Shoveling your driveway?"

Laughter filled the room. "You already do that without me asking, silly."

Yeah, he did, though he used the snowblower she had. Last year, the few storms they had in February, he'd shown up to help her, wanting to take some of the hard work off her back. She was constantly on the go, and he only wanted to help her in any small way he could. She'd never gotten angry at him for inserting himself into something that he didn't need to do—without even asking. Hell, he had even done her neighbor's driveway, Mr. Sheffield, a seventy-year-old widower who thanked him with a new hammer, even though he had several that worked fine. It was the thought that counted, and Cam appreciated the gesture, though it had been unnecessary. He would've plowed the driveway for nothing.

Before he could offer another bribe, her phone dinged. She swiped it so fast from the coffee table, he was surprised she didn't spill her drink in the process.

A heavy sigh released as a smile split across her lips. "They made it to Eric's. They had fun at the arcade."

Cam looked out her big bay window and watched as the snow came down in sheets. Thank goodness the boys made it their father's safely. He wasn't looking forward to driving in it himself.

"I'm so glad to hear that. Did they have fun while they were there?"

She nodded without looking up, her fingers tapping like mad on the screen. "They did. Royce won a football from the crane machine. They're going to play some video games now." Her phone made a loud plunking sound when she set it back on the coffee table. "I can now sleep better tonight."

He sure in the hell wasn't going to. Every night was the same as the others. Dreams of Serenity that he feared would never come true.

Her eyes glided to the bay window like he had. "It's really coming down."

"It is. I should go soon. Before it gets any worse."

He should have called her on his way and told her the roads weren't pleasant. But after a long week of not talking to her, he had to see her. To reassure himself they were good. Maybe not like they were a few weeks ago with no weird tension between them, but still friends, at least. He needed her in his life any way he could get her.

"Right. You should. Of course, I'll worry about you until you get home. Make sure you text me you made it okay."

Always the mother. Always the worrywart. One of the many things he loved about her.

"You know I will."

They finished most of their drinks, both having a few sips left in their glasses. An awkward chuckle filtered between them when they stood up at the same time.

"You can leave your glass here. I'll clean up."

He nodded and set his glass on the table next to the bottle of scotch. He wondered if she'd have more once he left. The thought saddened him because he wanted to finish the bottle with her.

She licked her lips. He released a sigh. They stared at each other for the longest time before he twisted around and headed for the closet for his jacket. Standing around gawking at each other, letting the tension get thicker wasn't going to solve anything, only make it worse.

He shrugged on his coat, wondering how he could see her again tomorrow, but not wanting to push his luck either. They needed to ease their way back into an uncomplicated friendship. How in the hell would they do that? He wasn't sure yet. But maybe all they needed was time.

She walked him to the door, biting her top lip as he wound his scarf around his neck.

His nerves were bordering on two chaotic choices. For her to ask him to stay. For her to wish him a safe drive. If she asked him to stay, he wouldn't refuse her this time.

But heaven help him, he needed to. Until she offered more than just sex, he had to hold firm.

Right?

Or should he take what she offered and hoped she changed her mind down the road? That she would see how wonderful they could be together?

More than likely that would only set him up for heart-break and he'd already had his fair share of that in his lifetime.

"It looks bad out there."

He hadn't opened the door yet, but he knew what she meant. Based on their observations through the bay window, it didn't look pretty.

"I'll drive slowly. My truck will take good care of me."

She swiped another finger behind her ear, despite no hair in the way—again. At least her nerves were as jumbled as his.

"If I ask..." She licked her lips. "If I..." She cleared her throat.

"Hey." He reached forward and brushed a tender hand down her cheek, then retreated, not sure he should've touched her. His resolve was barely hanging on. "It's okay, whatever you want to say. Ask away."

Ask me to stay. Now he wanted it with every breath in his body, even if it would be only sex. Damn his body for not agreeing with his mind.

"This is hard for me, Cam."

He unwrapped his scarf and unzipped his coat, but didn't take either off. Not yet. Then he moved in closer, aching to touch her, but resisted. Not yet.

"If you ask me to stay, I will."

There. He did it for her. Because despite her saying it was hard for her, it was difficult as hell for him as well. But someone had to do it. Since she put herself out there last time, he figured it was his turn.

"Then what?" she asked.

That was a loaded question and he didn't know where to start.

"Then we take it one moment at a time. All I know is I need you in my life, Serenity. Whether that's as friends, so be it. If it's as more, even better. But what I can't handle is not having you in my life. This past week was hell. I missed you more than I can possibly say."

Her hand reached forward and grabbed the end of his scarf, pulling until it was free. It fell to the floor. Her hands then glided inside his jacket near his shoulders, pulling down until that also came loose and fell to the floor.

Her eyes roamed his chest. The cream sweater he chose for the evening fit him well, no baggy parts to be had. Then her hands took the path her eyes had taken. First to his chest, then down south, stopping short of his jeans and snaking around until they were nestled behind his back. He stepped closer, wrapping his arms around her as well.

Her head fell forward, her ear pressing to his chest, and a relaxed sigh—for the first time that night—released.

"I need you too. That's what scares me the most."

He knew that feeling all too well. Because she felt it too, he had no idea where to go from here.

6

———————

"THIS BLOWS. I might join your side of Christmas sucks balls."

Serenity laughed hard at her sister and rolled her eyes. "I have never said that."

"Pretty damn close and you know it."

Whatever. So she didn't like the holiday most people enjoyed. She wasn't going to apologize for her feelings. Not that she ever let anyone know besides her sister. Honestly, her sister should hate it right along with her. Why was she alone in this hatred?

She grabbed another clear plastic ornament and started tying a red bow to the top. Her fingers were already aching from cutting the ribbon and tying the bows to the ornaments that were meant for the family Christmas party—her and Opal's duty that their mother assigned them. Everyone always had a task, and usually every year she and her sister were stuck on craft duties. Not that she'd ever complain. It was better than being stuck making cookies. Her mother knew how terrible she was with baking. Opal wasn't any better.

They had to make forty ornaments. Cut strips of paper. Of course, a multitude of colors so when they put the strips of paper inside the balls, it would look colorful. Everyone liked picking a different color. She always picked purple because it felt like the least Christmassy color of them all. Every year, each person grabbed one strip and wrote down one thing they were grateful for from the past year. After they finished eating, everyone took an ornament from the tree from last year, read the saying inside, and hung up a new one for next year to read aloud. It was, as her mother put it, a good way to remind each other that no matter what happened throughout the year, there was always something to be grateful for. All anyone ever needed was a reminder of such things. No one ever put their names on the ornaments either, so you never knew who wrote what. Unless you read a person's face well, and generally, everyone was able to figure out who wrote what. It wasn't hard to read face's when the culprit would giggle or smile wide at a particular phrase.

It was Serenity's favorite part about the party. She had an inkling why her mother created the tradition seven years ago; she just hated preparing for it. Cutting, tying, and sometimes nicking her finger on the top metal part of the ornament aggravated her. After so many years of doing it, one would think she'd be better at it. Not hurt herself so much.

Though it didn't help she had a teeny, tiny hangover from last night. A headache hovering at the edge of her forehead but not quite making its appearance known. Two cups of coffee and some aspirin had helped to keep it at bay. Hopefully, it stayed that way.

"So?"

Serenity resisted rolling her eyes again, lest her sister see. More ammunition to give her.

Opal groaned with impatience, set her latest ball down in the basket they had half-full, and stared intently at her. As if that would get her to break.

And damn her sister, it always did.

"So nothing happened. He spent the night, but we fell asleep on the couch together and that was that."

"You asked that man to stay the night and you didn't take him immediately to your bedroom."

"I didn't exactly ask him to stay."

She had chickened out, not wanting to be rejected again. He had asked for her. The entire conversation had been odd and left her with too many questions and not enough answers.

"I need details. I saw him leave this morning. And you haven't given me anything yet. I. Need. Details."

"It was snowing pretty badly last night. It was a good thing he stayed. He almost left, but he didn't, and we sat down on the couch and damn near finished off the bottle of scotch he brought over. We passed out on the couch together. There is literally nothing else to add to that."

Other than they sat so close together for the first time, thigh to thigh, her body had been so taut with tension, she almost jumped him on her couch. But she didn't. Because, though he stayed, she knew what he wanted. He had told her.

Not just sex.

She wasn't sure she could give him more. She already felt stupid enough asking for just sex. Cam deserved better than that. The last thing she wanted to do was ruin their friendship. Bringing sex into the mix would ruin it. He was right, even if it was hard to admit. Sex sounded so nice. She hadn't had any in quite a long time. That's what happened when you were a single mother and leery about bringing a new man around your boys. She was very cautious when it came to dating. Despite throwing sex on the table between them, she didn't have random sex. Like him, she wanted it to mean something.

So why in the hell had she thrown sex in his face like she had?

What a hypocrite!

"I know I asked this already, and you gave me no answer. What are you so afraid of?"

Serenity's hand paused tying another bow. Her entire life, at least from the moment she met Eric to the moment he left, flashed before her eyes.

"Risking my heart and losing it again."

Opal snorted. "Please, Eric was never worth your time. That was a mistake, and the only reason I don't remind you of that more is because that piece of shit gave you two wonderful boys. Cam is nothing like Eric."

Her sister was never shy about what she thought. Sometimes, Serenity appreciated it, other times, not so much. She didn't like to be reminded of the one colossal mistake she made in life. Falling for the wrong man. As always, she was also correct in saying he gave her the best thing ever. Two beautiful boys.

"It might've been a mistake, but at the time, I loved him. I poured everything I had into making it work with him. What was I left with? Nothing. Raising two boys on my own, basically."

"And you think Cam would do the same to you?"

She added her ornament to the pile and shrugged. "I'd like to think he wouldn't. I believe he'd never cheat on me. I know how much that hurt him. Of course, Eric never cheated on me either. That was never one of his many faults."

"That you know of."

Ugh. She wished her sister would've kept that to herself. Eric hurt her in so many ways; she wanted to believe he didn't hurt her in all the ways possible. And if he had cheated, that made her a fool because she had never found the evidence to say otherwise.

"Did you invite him to the party?"

"Yes, okay," Serenity said with a laugh, throwing the spool of ribbon at her sister, who caught it with ease. The smirk Opal sent her made more laughter slip out. "I was many cups into the scotch, as was he, so I don't even know if he remembers me asking him. I barely remember."

"Oh, he won't forget that. I won't let him."

"Stay away from him."

She did *not* need her sister meddling in her love life. If she wanted to call what was developing between her and Cam along the lines of a love life. She wasn't ready to admit she loved the man. Was she?

No, of course not. He was a good friend of hers. She appreciated and valued their friendship. That was all.

And, of course, she wanted to jump his bones.

Lust, not love.

"I can't. My sister needs me."

"I need you to not interfere."

"Last time I didn't interfere, you married the world's biggest jackass. This time, I will interfere if you screw this up."

Her sister wasn't wrong in that aspect either. She'd been screwing up left and right lately with Cam. Maybe she did need a little help. To get her head out of her ass and say the right thing for once.

"Are you seeing him again today? You have the whole

weekend free. No boys. No commitments. Clear agenda. Perfect time for sex."

Serenity shook her head, barely holding a snort back, not wanting to give her sister another angle to push the sex topic. Not that it would stop her. Opal would keep nagging her until she felt satisfied she got the result she was looking for. "It didn't come up. I offered breakfast and he said he had to get going. I left it at that."

"Ugh. I could scream at you right now. Seriously?"

Serenity's eyes widened in disbelief. "What did you want me to do? Tie him to my bed and say he can't leave? I offered breakfast and he declined."

"Yes, you should've tied him up last night. Kept him there all weekend long and did dirty, nasty things to him."

A combination of a laugh and a snort escaped from her lips. She couldn't hold in that snort no matter how hard she tried. Her sister was one to talk. It's not like she had an active sex life at the moment.

"He's—"

Her sister squealed with too much excitement when Serenity's phone rang, picking it up. "He's calling you right now. It's a sign from the gods. What I say is true. You need to get down and dirty with this man. As soon as possible."

Before Serenity could snatch her phone, Opal answered. "Hey there, stranger. Long time, no talky. I hear you're coming to our family Christmas party. It's the best. So much eggnog, you're gonna puke."

Serenity waved her hand impatiently at Opal to hand the phone over, scowling and giving her the fiercest motherly look she had in her arsenal. Her boys never defied her when she gave *the* look.

Unfortunately, Opal didn't even blink or cower in fear.

"You are hilarious, Cam. I adore you. Of course, Serenity adores you more. She has been wanting to—"

"Hey, Cam," Serenity said breathlessly, grabbing the phone from Opal before she could further embarrass her, almost scratching her hands in the process. She wasn't sorry about that either. Her sister was so in for it when she got off the phone. "You know how she gets when she's had three cups of coffee. The insanity comes out."

His smooth laughter set her heart on fire and her nerves jangling with need. So much need.

"She is a hoot. Always enjoy chatting with her. Though she didn't finish her sentence. What have you been wanting, Serenity?"

So much. Too much.

Not that she could confess anything with her sister staring at her like she was watching a movie marathon of all the 90s heartthrob movies that plucked at a young girl's heart.

"You can tell me. Tell me what you want."

CAM DAMN near held his breath waiting for Serenity to tell him what she wanted, but he didn't. He'd turn blue and die from lack of oxygen if he did that. He'd been wanting her to spill her feelings for a long time, had even given her a chance last night after laying some of his feelings on the table, and... nothing. She didn't give him a scrap of her feelings.

"I want..." Her voice trailed off as he swore he heard her hush her sister. Cam couldn't help but smile, wondering what Opal was whispering to her.

"I can call you back later. You two sound busy."

"No, it's okay. We're almost done. My fingers need a break anyway."

His brows pinched together. "What are you doing?"

She giggled, the sound lifting his spirits from the disappointment she still hadn't admitted what she truly wanted from him. "Making ornaments for the party. If you can't make it, I get it."

Well, if his memory was decent—and they had a lot to drink so he wouldn't be surprised if some of it was iffy—the party was next weekend. Same as the party Hope was throwing.

"Yeah, I can make it." Nothing would stop him from getting to spend more time with her. Not even a party his best friend was throwing. Mase would understand. "Hope and Mase were having a thing too, but this family Christmas party sounds intriguing. I don't want to miss out on the fun."

"Oh, shit, are they having a party next weekend?"

Obviously, Hope hadn't gotten around to inviting her yet.

He heard her snap her fingers.

"I completely spaced it out. She sent me a text about it and I said I'd be there. I didn't even double-check the day."

He hated how the stress poured out in each word. As if Hope and Mase would be mad at her for missing it. Serenity had always been a people-pleaser, never wanting to let anyone down. They would understand. Family came first. Mase knew how much he cared about Serenity, so he couldn't imagine Mase being pissed at him for missing it either.

"What time does the family party start?" Cam asked.

"The party always shifts every year from house to house. This year is at our parents' house. Mom wanted us girls

there at five to help get a few things set up. The party officially doesn't start until six."

"That works perfect. Hope and Mase's party starts
around two. We'll go there first, and then your parents'. How
does that sound?"

Her moment of hesitation had him thinking she didn't
like his idea. "Okay, we can do that."

"Good. Glad we got that settled."

"Was that the reason you called?"

It wasn't, but he had gotten sidetracked—since the
moment her sister answered the phone. But better to deal
with Opal over the phone than in person. He barely escaped
this morning.

He still felt bad how he darted out of the door with such
a quick good-bye, though he had shoveled her driveway. Not
that he wouldn't have regardless, but he had been forced to
in order to get his truck out of the driveway. She had offered
breakfast, and he declined like he regretted staying the
night. So far from the truth.

His stomach had been roiling with such unease, he
hadn't wanted to embarrass himself. The toilet had been
calling his name. It'd been a long time since he had drunk
so much that he wanted to puke the next morning. The
thought of food had sent him into a panic. Since he got
home, emptied his stomach, took a long hot shower, and
nibbled on some crackers, then a cup of coffee, he felt much
better. No headache, no stomachache, no aftereffects from
the night before. Of course, he didn't want to tell Serenity all
of that. But he did want to apologize.

"No, I wanted..." Back to the wanting conversation. Of
course, this time about the things he wanted. No point in
continuing to deny what he wanted. If she hadn't understood exactly where he stood last night, he figured now was

a good time to make it clearer. "I want to spend the day with you. But if you have plans with Opal, I get it. I'm last minute here so—"

"I'd love to spend the day with you."

Thank goodness she had cut him off. He only would've embarrassed himself further with his word vomit.

"Great. That's great."

Shut up, Cam. While you're ahead of the game.

"Let me finish these ornaments and then we can meet up. What did you have in mind?"

His eyes glided to the sleigh sitting in front of him.

"Nothing too much. How about I cook us supper?"

Most times, they hung out at her house. Serenity had been to his house a handful of times, but not for very long. Plus, if he was ever going to give her the sleigh, he had to just do it. Get it over with before he chickened out completely.

"Supper sounds nice. I'll be over in another hour or so."

The call ended with more awkwardness than he would've liked, but what could he do about it? He'd told her how he felt last night.

All I know is I need you in my life, Serenity. Whether that's as friends, so be it. If it's as more, even better.

That was pretty clear, he thought. But maybe he needed to be more specific with her. Tell her straight out he wanted to date her. Not only sex.

Though she might not want sex anymore. He'd stayed last night expecting something to happen, and all that happened was them sitting on the couch drinking the scotch and passing out. He figured she'd make the first move, but she could've been waiting for him to make it.

Damn it.

He was such an idiot.

Of course, he was treading new waters here. It'd been so long since he jumped back into the dating game—for real. Not minor dates where he knew he wouldn't go any further. After Melanie cheated on him, he'd been more cautious about women. Way more cautious.

So cautious, he rarely dated.

Now he was putting his heart back on the line and she wasn't taking the bait.

He blew out a breath and then cringed. The workshop was a mess. Not that he expected them to hang out in here, but if he found the courage to finally show her the sleigh, it needed to be more put together. Tools were hanging around everywhere. On the table, on the bench, some even taking a spot on the floor. The garbage can was overflowing, and the counters had empty beer bottles that made it look like he drank too much. He didn't. A beer every now and again. Only problem was, he had a bad habit of not cleaning up.

His house didn't look much better. And shit. He only had a little over an hour to clean up two places, take another shower because he knew he'd work up a sweat fixing everything, and scour his fridge for a decent meal. If he didn't have the correct food, he'd have to run to the grocery store as well.

Not enough time.

He was so screwed.

7

THE WINE BOTTLE twisted in her hands as she blew out a tiny breath and made her way up the walkway. They had a lot to drink last night and having another drink was the last thing they should do, but she couldn't come empty-handed.

Cam had done a great job shoveling. At her house too. She had yet to say thank you for him doing that. It had been one less job for her. He had rushed out so fast this morning, she barely had a chance to say anything to him.

She had taken longer than a simple hour to make it to his house. More like two and a half. She had sent a text and he had reassured her it was okay, to take her time. So she had. Her closet and bedroom were now a complete mess, but after painstakingly going through a bajillion outfits, she found the right one. She hoped so anyway. One of her comfiest pairs of jeans, which also happened to make her butt look good. So her sister had told her. She didn't have a habit of looking at her butt because she always thought it was too big. At least, when she went shopping for jeans and the size she always wanted never fit right. Too snug in too many places. She had paired it with a blue blouse that wasn't snug, but it showed off her cleavage pretty well.

Cam wouldn't mind what she wore. He always complimented her, no matter the clothes she had on.

But she wanted to look good. She wanted...

She blew out another breath before ringing the doorbell.

The door opened a few seconds later with Cam dressed in a soft tan sweater and one of her favorite pairs of jeans he owned. His ass looked so delicious in it. His smile said he was ecstatic to see her. Even though she might ignore her own butt, she didn't hesitate to check his out. Not that she ever let him know she was.

She knew what she wanted. She was just afraid to say it out loud. Hell, even think it to herself.

She wanted this man with every breath in her body, and it scared the living daylights out of her.

"Come on in. I swear the temps are dropping again like it wants to dump more snow on us," Cam said with laughter as he gestured her inside.

She shivered, unsure whether it was from agreeing with his assessment or the fact he placed his hand on her back after closing the door. If he noticed the moment of edginess when he took the bottle of wine from her, he didn't say anything. When she removed her coat, he took that as well.

"I can hang it up."

His smile brightened, confusing her and exciting her for some odd reason. The sexual tension that had been simmering and building between them was burning hot and steamy right now. Every movement he made, every tiny gesture set her body on fire. It shouldn't. The way she was reacting was ridiculous. This was Cam. Her good friend Cam. The guy always there for her in every possible way. If anything, she was a terrible friend because she took advantage of that knowledge, leaning on him more than she should.

"Relax. Tonight I pamper you."

Oh, yes, please!

She giggled, then snorted, embarrassing herself further when he looked at her funny as if he didn't understand the joke. There was no joke, only her erratic thoughts that needed to get it together.

"As if I pampered you last night or something. I didn't do much." *I didn't do anything. Like jump your bones as I should've, according to my sister. Now stop thinking sexual thoughts!*

"You're always working so hard, Serenity. Let me take the load on for once."

She nodded, not because she agreed, because she didn't mind everything she had to do. It was a part of her life. Making sure the boys had everything they needed, kept them on track and in a good routine. Helping her mother when she needed her, same for her sister. She was a busybody, and she didn't mind that title. If people needed her, she helped. Being needed felt good. Because what was she if she wasn't needed? Not something she wanted to think about.

No, she nodded because it was a refreshing feeling to know someone else could do the same for her. Would *want* to do the same for her.

He hung her coat up with swift hands, then jerked his head toward his kitchen. She smiled at the cozy fireplace already lit in his living room and sighed happily when they walked into the kitchen. He set the bottle of wine on the counter and grabbed two wine glasses from a cupboard.

"Something smells good."

A crockpot sat on the counter, the lid filled with condensation on the inside. The rich aroma filled the entire kitchen and had even lingered in the foyer. Now that she was closer to it, she thought she smelled a bit of barbecue flavor in the air. She wanted to scoot closer and inhale deeply but didn't want to look funny. She'd already embarrassed herself enough and she hadn't been here a full five minutes yet.

"Pulled pork?"

The way he said it questioningly and with a slight wince said he was nervous about what she'd think about it.

"It smells divine. I can't wait to try it."

"Well, it's going to take a while still. Another few hours, but it is a specialty in my family, so I do hope you like it. I have fixings for a salad, and I thought some mashed potatoes and broccoli on the side would be nice. Though we can change that. Whatever you want to eat. We don't even have to have pulled pork. I bought this bruschetta bread to go with it, but—"

She stepped forward, brushing her finger over his lips, silencing him. The nerves she felt on the drive over, the way they intensified when she pulled into the driveway and shot off like a rocket when he opened the door finally calmed. Because knowing he was as nervous as her was a blessing. They were in this together. Whatever the hell this was.

Her finger slid away.

"Everything sounds wonderful. I don't know how long I can wait to try the pork, it seriously smells so good. And I'm wondering why you've never made it for me before."

He shrugged. "We don't hang out at my house as much as yours."

Very true. Because normally the boys were home and it

was easier to be at her house. Coming to his house signified something more. Something different. She had never wanted to mess with that, especially with the boys. Not that she feared they'd hate it if she started dating Cam. They already loved him.

Silence developed between them when she didn't respond right away. Their gazes held, the small space between them filling with anticipation that'd been building for too long now. She licked her bottom lip and his eyes followed.

"So what do we do while we wait for the food?" The way the question came out more breathlessly than she intended told him what she wanted.

But why hide it? Why were they still resisting each other? They should get the sexual tension out of the air and everything would go back to normal. They'd be the best of friends and life would go on.

Even she knew that was a lie, but it was a lie she'd continue to tell herself until she had no choice but to face the truth.

"I have something for you. Would you like to see it?" He swallowed hard, his Adam's apple bobbing nervously.

Was this the mysterious Christmas present he had mentioned? Not that she wanted a present, especially one for Christmas, but perhaps it was better to get it out of the way. Then she wouldn't have to think about it anymore.

"Sure."

He grabbed her hand and pulled her toward the back door. She'd taken her shoes off by the front door, but he had an extra pair of boots for her to slip on. They were obviously heading to his workshop outside in the backyard. They ran down the path, her boots clomping on the ground, especially since they were several sizes too large. The coldness seeped through her since they hadn't thrown on a jacket, but his hand still wrapped around hers kept the warmth in.

When he opened the door and she stepped into his workshop, more warmth hit her senses.

Her eyes bulged at the sight of the large sleigh sitting in the middle of the room.

That couldn't be it?

Could it?

The way his hand trembled in hers said it was.

"Merry Christmas. I figured someone who loves Christmas as much as you should have the best sleigh in town."

Oh, God.

She should tell him the truth.

Her hand slid out of his as she walked forward to get closer. She was in awe of his craftsmanship. The details, the carvings, the perfection.

It was too much.

Everything was just too much.

CAM WAITED for Serenity to say something. Her back was to him while she inspected the sleigh, yet no sounds came out. Not even an exclamation of surprise. Nothing.

She hated it.

It was too much. He shouldn't have gone so big. Something smaller would've been much better. What the hell had he been thinking?

She climbed into the sleigh and sat down. He couldn't even see her anymore.

Then her head popped out, a short smile on her face, though he didn't see it glimmering in her eyes. She definitely hated it.

"Come up here. This seat is so comfortable."

He knew that. It took him forever to find the perfect cushion for the bench inside. Not that he expected her to sit forever on it, but if she chose to, he wanted it to be comfortable. He was glad she thought so.

He grabbed a hold of the side and pulled himself up and took a seat next to her. Her hand grasped his as soon as his thigh touched hers.

"This must've taken you a long time to build."

"I enjoyed doing it. I like building things."

A cold hand hit his cheek, then slight pressure for him to turn and look at her. He was afraid to do so, but he didn't resist. The sparkle in her eyes was a little easier to decipher being this close to her. Not hatred. Not happiness, though. Apprehension, maybe?

"It was too much, wasn't it? I wanted to—"

Her lips were suddenly on his, quieting whatever word vomit that would've spilled out this time. He wasn't going to miss this opportunity again. Or screw it up by letting his fear win.

He let go of her hand to wrap his arms around her and pull her closer. His tongue dove in, taking control of the kiss. She let him, moaning in delight when his hands squeezed her waist.

Then she was shifting until she was straddling his lap, her hands smoothing up his cheeks and through his hair.

Oh, God, he couldn't take much more. He was hard as a rock and his cock was begging to be let out, especially when she kept grinding lightly into him. He bit her bottom lip, soothing it with his tongue, then trailed kisses down her chin, across her neck, to her ear.

"I need you, Serenity."

She leaned back, taking her sweater off and tossing it to the side. His eyes glided to her breasts that were trapped in a red lacy bra that needed to disappear.

"I need you more, Cam."

He grinned as his fingers went for the clasp in the back. "Are we about to argue who needs the other more?"

Her hands, which were warming up by the second, grabbed the edges of his sweater, brushing back and forth across his stomach before yanking it up and over his head. That sailed across the room like hers had.

"No arguing. Only feeling."

"I can manage that." Then her bra was free and his mouth was claiming a pert nipple begging for attention.

From there, no more sounds echoed between them but moans and low growls he couldn't keep in when she would shift a certain way on his lap. He was ready to explode and he hadn't even removed his pants yet.

He took his time savoring the perfection in front of him —in case this didn't happen again. They had gone from small talk to intensity in the blink of an eye. Was this just sex? Was this more?

Even not knowing the correct answer, he didn't stop. He'd take what she was offering and worry about the consequences later.

Her hands unbuttoned his jeans, and he knew he wouldn't last long. It'd been a while since he'd been with a woman.

She stood up, kicked off her boots, then removed her jeans and panties that matched her bra. He did the same, grabbing a condom from his wallet before rolling it on. Luck had been on his side that he forgot to toss his wallet in the junk drawer when he got home from the grocery store. Running inside the house for a condom would've ruined the moment.

His hands palmed her waist and drew her closer. The sweet, sensual smile on her face had his cock twitching and his heart galloping. Damn, he wanted this woman for the rest of his life, and he knew if he uttered one word in that direction, she'd run from him.

Her knees straddled his legs, then cupping his cock, he positioned himself and she sat down, her head tossing back as the bliss spread across her face.

"Oh, Cam," she said breathlessly, her head falling forward when she was buried deep to the hilt. Her lips hit his neck sending a shockwave of ecstasy coursing through his body. "It's been so long."

"Same," he whispered, his hands tightening on her thighs. Partly to stop the pressure from building too soon, and partly to get ready to pump hard. "Ride me."

She lifted her head and giggled. "That was so cheesy. I love it."

He chuckled with her, glad to have calmed himself down so he could enjoy it for more than a few seconds. He hadn't meant for that to come out like it had, but it helped. And hell, they were in a sleigh. It'd be the only time it got a ride this intense.

They smiled together before she started gliding up and down. He tightened his hold and pumped hard with her. Heat built, and the tension that had swirled between them for the longest time finally snapped and broke free.

He couldn't take it any longer and he tensed, the pleasure taking a hold of him. Her sweet cries that filled the air said she came along with him.

Her head rested on his shoulder as they both slowly came down from the high.

His lips trailed small kisses on her neck, but he held in any words. Because the things he wanted to say would ruin the moment. And he wanted this magic to stay for as long as possible.

8

"Okay, I don't care how I have to convince you, but I need this recipe." Serenity made sure to use her brightest, sexiest smile she owned because the pulled pork was the best she ever had. She could not leave without the recipe.

Cam smirked behind his sandwich, sauce dripping onto his plate. "Bold words. It might take a lot of convincing. It's a secret family recipe. I can't share it with anyone."

Her mind, which she imagined was the intention, swirled back to the sleigh and the amazing things he made her feel. She'd never had sex anywhere but in a bed. Thinking about her dull sex life made her feel pathetic. In the beginning, dating Eric, they had sex all the time. They never had a problem in that department; it was everything else that fell apart. Despite their active activities in the bedroom, it never actually occurred outside of a bedroom. Since Eric, she didn't date a whole lot as a single mother, and when she did, she usually didn't bring the man home; she went to his place. Where sex happened in a bed.

Now that she'd experienced something so new and refreshing—and a bit naughty in her mind—she wanted to do it again and again and again. With Cam, of course. So if he wanted her to convince him, she had no problem doing that.

Here on the table, for starters.

A giggle let loose as the thought whirled through her mind.

"This is serious business. No laughing." Though the humor in Cam's eyes said he was laughing with her.

Except he didn't know what she was finding humorous.

"What different kinds of places have you had sex before?"

Cam coughed, choking on the bite he had taken. It took him a while to calm down and clear his throat.

"A little warning before you jump into that kind of conversation." His lips stretched wide as the laughter in his eyes increased. "Like weird places? Do you think it's odd we had sex in the sleigh?"

"Oh, I loved it." She reached out and touched the top of his hand. "I've...it's embarrassing, but I've never had sex outside of a bed. I'm curious."

Cam twisted his hand until he had hers gripped within his, and brought it to his mouth, planting a kiss on top of it.

"It is now my life's mission to make sure you have sex in the most random places."

More giggles slipped out, images flashing before her of the kind of places he might have in mind.

"You didn't answer my question."

He shrugged. "A hot tub. A bathtub. The living room. A closet on campus that I swear we were going to get caught. The men's locker room on campus that I also swore we'd get caught."

They laughed together.

The joy in his eyes dimmed. "All with Melanie. So I can't

say they are happy memories anymore. It kind of makes me sick to think about. I did some dumb stuff with her, and for what? For her to go behind my back and pretend my feelings didn't matter."

Cam still held her hand. She squeezed in comfort, though didn't say anything. Anything she said wouldn't take his pain away. She only knew that because, no matter what anyone said about Eric, it didn't erase her pain. The regret she wasted so many years on him.

"So if I want to have sex on this table later, we can?"

Cam snorted, obviously shocked by her response. Instead of giving him comfort that wouldn't help, she turned the moment back into joy. At least, that was her goal.

"Anything for you, Serenity. And I'll never say no to sex."

The moment he said the words, silence stretched across the room. Because he had previously said no to sex. To her. Not that she was going to point it out, and he didn't either.

He cleared his throat. "And I hope we can have some in my bed too. That's if...you want to spend the night. I'd like that."

Spend the night? With Cam? She hadn't slept with a man all night long in too many years. She'd gotten used to having a bed to herself. No one to hog any part of it. No one to snatch the covers away. No one snoring and keeping her awake.

If she spent the night, didn't that signify they were something more than...well, whatever they were now. She wasn't sure she was ready to define them.

Of course, if she left, she'd be going home to an empty house. Being here with Cam was something she wanted a lot more than an empty house.

"Okay, I'll spend the night." Her eyes grazed to her sandwich that was almost gone on her plate. "If I get the recipe."

She couldn't resist adding that.

The devilish smirk that lit up his features told her she hadn't offended him. That he understood she was joking.

"It might take all night to convince me of that." He let go of her hand and picked his sandwich back up. "Tomorrow we can take the sleigh to your house before the boys get home. They'll love to see it when they pull up to the house."

Right. The sleigh.

He must've sensed her hesitation about it because his smile slid away and neutral features hit his face. A touch of hurt as well.

"You don't like it."

"It's big." She laughed, hoping to douse the sudden tension. "I don't have anywhere to store it when Christmas is over."

He frowned. "I didn't think about that." Then he chuckled. "That was a huge lapse on my part."

She stood up and waited for him to scoot his chair back and sat on his lap, wrapping her arms around his neck. "I like the sleigh. The craftsmanship is amazing. I can tell how hard you worked on it. Now that we...christened it," she giggled, "I don't want to share it with anyone else. I don't want people in town to stop and comment and want to sit in it. It'll ruin what we shared. Can we keep it here?"

He looked serious for a moment, then a smile brightened his lips. "Of course. Makes total sense." Then he nodded toward the table behind her back. "So about that sex on the table..."

"Yes. Keep talking."

"No, we're done talking."

Then his lips were on hers and nothing else mattered. Not even the tiny tension she still felt in his shoulders and lingering in the air.

It wasn't about the sleigh, even though it seemed like it.
She hated Christmas.

Soon, she should confess it, so he understood.

———

SHE TRIED NOT to let her irritation show as she exited the car, but it was hard when she saw the sad look on Randall's face as he exited his father's vehicle.

"Where were you?" Eric demanded as if he had a right to know her whereabouts.

"You weren't going to drop them off until six. Why so early?"

If he thought she was going to march to his tune, he was so wrong. She was done being his little puppet, something he should've figured out a long time ago.

"I have a work thing." Eric nodded his head toward the boys who were walking toward the garage without a good-bye. "I heard about some boy picking on Randall. He needs to man up and stop being such a wussy."

To think she had been having such a wonderful week-end, and for it to go from blissful to hatred in a second. Only something Eric was capable of. She saw Randall stiffen, while Royce punched in the code to the garage panel and walk inside once the door lifted.

She waited until they were out of earshot to lay into Eric.

"What did you say to him?"

"Shit he needed to hear. Stop coddling him like he's a baby. He needs to grow up."

She clenched her teeth, attempting to keep her anger in. No need to put on a show for the neighborhood, or her boys who could be looking out the window. Not Randall, though. He went to his room, she figured, like he always did when something bothered him. But Royce wasn't one to walk away. He'd eavesdrop to know what was going on.

"And you need to act like a father who gives a shit about his kids' feelings. Instead of getting angry at the boy picking on him, you get angry at him. Make that make sense. Because it doesn't."

"If he manned up—"

"Oh, enough of the man bullshit!" she seethed, taking a step closer, aching to slap him across the face for his ignorance. "Who are you to talk about what a man is? How a man should act? You're not even a damn man. You're the disgrace and the wussy. If you ever speak to my son like that again, you'll be sorry."

Then she stomped by him without another word or waiting for him to respond because she didn't trust herself not to lash out physically. His heated words that sliced the cold air behind her back didn't stop her. She had no desire to stick around to listen to the emptiness he wanted to spew. The garage door slid down and hit the ground with a large thump. His hollering finally drowned out.

She entered through the kitchen and found Royce waiting for her.

"I'm sorry, honey."

Royce shrugged. "I don't why I ever expect something different from him. We were having a good time until last night when we ran into Dawson's dad. He had things to say since you had confronted Dawson's mom."

She winced, not proud of herself for that.

"It kind of surprised me when dad took their side and not Randall's. It wasn't fun after that."

"Oh, sweetie." She set her purse on the counter and pulled him into a hug. "Why didn't you call me? I would've picked you both up."

Cam would've understood. Hell, she figured Cam would've even come with her to pick them up. He was more a father to her boys than their own was. Which said something because they weren't even dating—officially.

"I didn't want to give him more ammunition and call us babies." Royce backed away and walked to the fridge, pulling out a pop. "How was your weekend?"

That signified Royce didn't want to talk about it anymore. She didn't want to keep pushing the issue. Their father was an ass, and Royce knew it. What was left to say?

Well, telling her son she had a wonderful time with Cam didn't seem appropriate, or nice.

"It was okay. I missed you both. It's still pretty early. We should do something fun. I refuse to let this ruin the rest of your weekend."

Eric had called her before eight in the morning, waking her out of a good sleep, curled in Cam's arms to say he was bringing the boys home. She barely had time to wipe the sleep from her eyes before jumping into her car. Since she hadn't brought a change of clothes, not knowing she'd sleep over, she had to put last night's clothes on. Not that Eric or the boys would know that's what she had worn yesterday. For all they knew, she had run to the store for something. Even though she didn't have any bags with her.

She had left Cam in such a rush, she didn't even kiss him good-bye. But he understood. As soon as she mentioned the boys, he helped her gather her clothes and walked her to the door. Such a kind, caring man. So far from how Eric was.

Royce shrugged again. "Like what? We have school tomorrow so not much to do."

"Well," she started, not sure what they could do either, when it hit her. "There's a fresh coat of snow, and we missed the snowman building contest. Which would've been a prime time to play in it. Why don't we go snowboarding or something? Get that dose of snow in."

"Yeah, Richie talked about going to Dragon Hill this weekend. Maybe he'll be there."

Serenity wasn't a fan of Dragon Hill because of how steep, bumpy, and curvy it was. She'd rather go somewhere else, but with his excitement and the light back in his eyes, how could she say no? Maybe even Randall would get out of his funk as well. She hated when he retreated to his room, even if he had a good excuse to feel down.

"Great. Let's have breakfast. I'll make waffles. Then afterward, we'll head there and you two can work on your skills."

Because they were still pretty amateur, but once her boys started practicing something, they worked at it until they were pros. They loved sports and being outdoors, and if they weren't glued to some kind of electronic device, she called that a win.

"Cool. I'll go tell Randall." Royce turned, then stopped. "Hey, do think Cam would want to go with us?"

"Ummm...do you want him to come with?"

Royce nodded. "Yeah, there's a trick I've been wanting to try, and he could teach us. He knows how to snowboard. You don't, Mom."

This was true. She didn't even buy herself one because the thought scared her. She was terrible at skiing. But last year for Christmas she had bought both of them a snowboard because she knew they'd enjoy it. No sense taking their joy away just because the thought scared her.

"I'll give him a call."

"Cool. Thanks!" Then he rushed out of the room with even more excitement.

She took off her jacket and shoes, pulled the waffle

maker out, then dialed her phone while she grabbed the ingredients she needed. Cam answered on the first ring.

"Is everything okay? The boys good?"

The smile that spread across her face made the hurt and anger filling her up inside dissipate a shred. He was such a good man. So kind and loving. How disappointing that Eric couldn't be the same with his own kids.

"Things could be better. Eric's being a colossal ass again. I suggested snowboarding and that brightened up Royce. I haven't even chatted with Randall yet. Sometimes, Royce gets through to him better than I can."

Cam cleared his throat before asking, "What did he do? Do you want to talk about it?"

Not really. But if where they were going was into relationship territory, she should want to talk about these things with him. He wasn't just going into a relationship with her, he was taking on her boys too. He never once let her doubt how much he cared about her boys as much as he cared about her.

"He ran into Dawson's dad. Apparently, Eric thinks Randall needs to man up. Like he knows how a man acts. I wanted to hit him. Or spit at him. Unleash all this anger at him for hurting the boys like that. They didn't have fun, needless to say."

"I'm sorry to hear that. I'm sorry he's so blind to how wonderful they are."

"So, do you want to go snowboarding with us? Royce wants to learn a new trick. Though nothing too crazy I hope."

Cam's laughter filled more of her heart with joy. "We'll be super careful, Mom, I promise."

She knew a day by his side, she'd forget the incident with Eric with ease. What a wonderful idea by Royce.

"You better," she teased in return. "I don't want any broken bones."

"Where should I meet you?"

She looked at all the ingredients sitting on the counter. "I'm making waffles. We never did have breakfast this morning. Why don't you join us and we'll ride together. You can alleviate my fears of Dragon Hill, which is where Royce wants to go."

Cam blew out a breath and a short chuckle. "Do you have any of that scotch left? A shot before we leave might alleviate some of your fears."

"That is not helping, Cam."

More laughter filtered through. "I'll be right over. I lo— can't wait to hang out with you and the boys today."

"I can't wait either."

In an instant, her annoyance and frustration changed with one simple phone call. Cam made their world better.

They should have a talk soon. About them. About putting a label on what was developing between them. Because that *just sex* business was silly. She should've never said such a thing in the beginning. She should've realized nothing could be *just sex* with Cam. He deserved better, and so did she.

9

CAM HAD his hand raised to knock when the door flew open. The excitement in Royce's eyes was enough to know whatever had happened with his dad couldn't have been too bad. Or maybe he was pushing it down and ignoring it. Cam knew that feeling all too well.

"Mom said we can go to Dragon Hill. She said you can teach us all the cool tricks."

"I'll do my best. I heard she's making waffles first."

Royce nodded, then shut the door behind him. "Randall will be out soon. Maybe you can stick around after and play those video games like you said you would."

Cam knew Royce wasn't testing him and how trustworthy he could be, but it still felt like a test. He knew Royce's father had let him down too many times. If there was one thing he would never do—or do his damndest to try—was not let these boys down.

"Of course. As long as your mom doesn't mind."

Royce waved his hand in the air as if saying 'give me a break'. "You know she loves it when you come around. So do we. I like seeing my mom happy."

Then he was rushing out of the room when Randall hollered from another room in the house. Saved by a shout. He had no idea how to respond to that. A few weeks ago, Cam thought they were only friends. Now their relationship had entered new territory, and he was so afraid he was going to muck it up and lose her for good. That was the last thing he wanted to happen.

He took his shoes off, hung up his coat, and found Serenity in the kitchen looking divine in last night's clothes. The memory of their night flashed like a movie on fast-forward. He wanted to slow it down and relive each moment so he could cherish it again like he had last night.

She turned around from the counter, let out a little shriek, and giggled when she saw his crooked grin.

"You scared the shit out of me. I didn't hear you knock."

"Royce got to me before I could. Someone is very excited to go snowboarding."

The smile that spread across her face lit a fire in his gut. One that had to stay tamped down because no hanky-panky could go on with the boys around. At least, not yet. Not until they talked about where they were officially going with each other.

"No crazy tricks. This is their first time going since last season and they might be super rusty."

Cam walked around the island and stopped in front of her. Close enough to pull her into his arms, but he didn't. Not yet. "It's my first time too. I'm going to be a bit rusty. But it's like riding a bike. It'll come back with ease."

"I saw you snowboard last year. You're insanely good. You're being very modest right now."

He couldn't resist. The temptation was too much. His arm wrapped around her waist and pulled her close. "I'm trying to keep your worry at bay. I promise no broken bones."

Her hand fell to his chest, a mixture of a laugh and cry escaping. "There better not be any." Then her head dropped to his chest, her arms wrapping around him tight. "I hate Eric so much sometimes. Thank you for being here."

He planted a kiss on her head. "I'll always be here for you."

Her body jerked as if she heard a noise or something, and she pushed away from him, walking back to the counter where she'd been preparing the waffles. He tried not to let it affect him that she walked away so quickly, as if she didn't want the boys to see them embracing. Until they had a real talk, it was for the best the boys didn't see anything. It didn't mean it didn't hurt.

"I hope you're hungry."

"I'm starving, and those waffles smell delicious. I had coffee before you called, but that was about it."

Because the moment she woke up with a start, rushed to put her clothes on, and ran out of the house without even a good morning kiss, he'd been worried.

Worried about the boys.

Worried about her.

Worried about where they stood.

Like an idiot, he had almost confessed he loved her. Over the phone, no less. While he wanted to get it all out in the open, not doing it face-to-face wasn't something he wished. He might not be ready to lose her, but continuing any further without laying his heart on the line wasn't an option either. He'd spent too much of his life with Melanie thinking one thing was going to happen, and the complete opposite thing had. He wasn't about to waste his life repeating the same mistakes.

If she didn't love him in return or didn't think she ever could, then it was best to stop what they were doing and move on. Stay friends.

Or acquaintances. He wasn't sure he could still be her friend and stay as close as they were now that they had slept together.

"There's more coffee over there if you want some."

"Sure. Do you need more?" he asked as he ventured to the pot to pour himself a cup.

"I'm good, but the waffles are almost done. Go get the boys for me. We'll eat and hit the road."

"You got it." He made it to the doorway before turning around. "Royce mentioned playing some video games afterward. I hope you don't mind."

"You know I don't. Thank you for indulging them."

That bugged him. Rubbed him the wrong way, and he figured she hadn't meant to hurt him, but she had anyway.

"I don't indulge anyone here. I stay because I want to. I'm here because it's where I want to be. I'm in this one hundred percent with you. Not just caring about you, but about those boys. I thought you knew that."

Before he said anything he'd regret, like blurting out he loved her and the boys, he turned around and walked out.

Now was not the time to be having a serious conversation. Not with the boys in listening distance. He hadn't meant to say anything, but he couldn't let that stand. Those words hit him wrong. He needed her to know it wasn't okay.

He knocked on the doorframe to Randall's room where they both were hanging out, their winter gear all over the floor.

"Your mom says the waffles are almost done. Time for breakfast."

"You'll convince Mom that we can stay more than an

hour." Randall already had his knit hat on, and Cam figured if he could eat waffles with his gloves on, he would've put those on too.

These boys were ready to hit the slopes and skip breakfast.

"Well, you know she's not a fan of Dragon Hill. It can be dangerous. Hitting a bump in the wrong way can send you flying and landing badly. Don't go overboard and I think we can convince her to stay all morning. Maybe even make some hot chocolate to bring in a thermos."

"Thanks for coming with, Cam. Mom hates going snow-boarding. She won't even go on the skis she got two Christ-mas's ago," Randall replied. The happiness in his eyes didn't portray he just left his father who hadn't made him feel good.

"I love snowboarding. I'm game anytime."

He felt like he should say something else, something more, but he held back. It wasn't his place to talk to them about their dad, and he didn't want to overstep. Yet he wanted them to know he'd always be there for them. That they could always count on him, unlike their father.

But could they?

If Serenity kicked him out of her life, it wasn't as if he could still stay in their lives. That's not how it worked with exes. Whether labeled as an ex-boyfriend or an ex-friend. He couldn't keep hanging out with them and showing them some men could be dependable.

"So when are you going to ask out our mom, anyway, Cam? Isn't it time?" Royce popped out, staring at him with an intensity that scared him. More than the question itself did.

"I figured they were already dating. Cam's over here so

much it feels like it. You can kiss her in front of us if you want," Randall added.

"Yeah, but not too much. That's kind of weird. But sometimes." Royce shrugged and nodded at Randall, waiting for him to agree.

"Well?" Randall prompted.

"Yeah, well?" Royce joined in when Cam didn't respond.

Shit. What the hell was he supposed to say to that? Had they heard the thoughts creating chaos inside him? Was that why this conversation popped out of nowhere?

"So you two are cool if we date?"

"We wouldn't want to play video games and hang out as much as we do with you if we weren't. Why do you think we ask you as much as we do? A little help never hurts." The twinkle in Royce's eyes said this kid was a lot smarter than Cam gave him credit for.

"Thanks for that. You know I don't just stay for her. I like hanging out with you two as well."

Randall nodded. "We know that. We know fake, and you've never shown that to us."

Meaning they'd seen it from their dad. How sad. He wanted to confront the bastard himself and show him some pain for the hurt he put these boys through.

"Well, as long as you don't mind me hanging around a lot more, because I might be. Your mom even invited me to the family Christmas party next weekend."

"Oh, boy." Royce laughed with Randall. "Those can get crazy. Don't tell Mom, but we know she can't stand those parties."

He had no idea. When she mentioned it, she sounded excited about the prospect. "Too much family togetherness?"

"Oh, no. It's the Christmas festivities left and right. Mom hates Christmas."

Randall nodded in agreement. "She thinks she hides it from us, but we know."

Well, that was news to him. Cam had never once gotten the inkling she didn't like Christmas.

Was that why she didn't want the sleigh moved from his house? Was that why she didn't seem to love it as much as he thought she would?

Wow. He was an idiot, and so damn clueless. Why did he never see what was always right in front of him when it came to women?

"Why does she hate Christmas?"

Royce shared a look with Randall. "It's complicated and hard to explain. I'm glad you'll be at the party. Maybe she'll enjoy it for once."

"Yeah, without pretending," Randall added.

Cam hoped so. He and Serenity had a lot more to talk about than he realized.

His ears perked up when he heard her holler.

"Waffles are done and we better get our butts in gear. Hey, for now, let's keep this chat between us. But I'm glad I know I have your support. It means the world to me."

Royce and Randall smiled and with a quick nod confirmed their talk would remain silent.

For now.

Cam didn't want secrets between him and Serenity, so he'd eventually tell her. But first, she needed to share her secrets with him.

Like the fact she hated Christmas.

Here he was trying to woo her with the Christmas spirit and she despised the holiday. No wonder he'd been failing.

It wasn't pulling her closer to him, only sending the divide between them farther apart.

———

SHE CLOSED her eyes and willed her mind to think of positive thoughts. Then she opened them and her heart skipped a beat. Watching these three snowboard down this monstrosity wasn't helping her anxiety. She should've stayed in the car or something. Despite the frigid temperatures, she stayed at the bottom of the hill, watching them climb the beast, then board down it like they were born on the slopes. Only a few times watching and eyeing Cam like a hawk and her boys were pros like she knew they'd be. Of course, the few tricks—nothing too crazy, thankfully—Cam was showing them weren't too hard. He had promised her he wouldn't do anything too wild, and she knew she could count on him.

"Hey, you. Freezing your butt off yet?"

Serenity turned to Hope, who came out of nowhere and smiled for the first time since arriving at Dragon Hill over two hours ago. "I'm so cold I'm numb everywhere. I can't feel my fingers or toes."

Hope laughed, then passed her an extra coffee. Serenity offered her thanks and drank merrily, not even caring she burnt the roof of her mouth at first. She had brought a thermos of hot chocolate like the boys and Cam requested, but she hadn't touched it yet, wanting to save it for them. They had stopped only twice for a sip and to catch their breath. She had stood at the bottom of the hill, walking back and forth to keep her muscles loose and her feet from falling off from lack of boredom. They even suggested she could wait in the car, but she didn't want to. No matter how cold she got, she enjoyed watching her boys have fun. Even if it terrified her every time they went down the steep, bumpy hill.

"I didn't know Cam called Mase," Serenity said as she saw Mase making his way up the hill to meet the gang.

"He didn't. Mase texted him, and when Cam said what he was doing, he decided to join him. I came for moral support. Plus, I'm still irked by who won the snowman contest yesterday and I thought standing in the cold might cool my anger."

Serenity giggled. "Oh, dear, who won?"

"Marybeth. Can you believe it? That wretched woman doesn't even like walking on snow, so I can't believe she'd push it around to create a snowman. She teamed up with Jax. Honestly, I don't know what he sees in her."

Aww, the cute veterinarian who rarely dated around town. That was an odd choice for him to be dating Marybeth, the worst viper there was. She tried to get in every man's pants, married or not. It was sad.

"I'm sorry I missed that. I bet it was a sight to see."

"I was surprised not to see you and the boys. You rocked it last year."

"They were with their father this weekend. Which didn't go so well. Thank goodness we were able to come here and turn it around."

"Yeah, I know a thing or two about shitty fathers. I get it. Sorry to hear that. So will you and Cam be making the party next weekend?"

Serenity was grateful for the conversation change, even if Hope could resonate with her.

"In the beginning. I hope you don't mind we can't stay the entire time. My family's party is on that day as well. If I don't show up, my mom will disown me."

"Of course. It's kind of a last-minute thing. I've been in such a good mood since winning the election that celebrating sounded like fun. I have so many ideas for the town, I can't wait to get started."

"You're going to do amazing."

They continued chatting, a light cold breeze blowing, sipping their coffees, as all the boys snowboarded. Sometimes crashing like they were on wobbly feet, other times flying down the hill like they were competing in the Olympics.

Several hours later, they were all at Serenity's house trying to warm up. Cam and Mase were challenging the boys at video games in the living room, while she and Hope were getting food ready.

"You sure you don't mind we came over too?" Hope asked as she spread mayo on a slice of bread.

They decided to make sandwiches and have some chips. Something light, since it was past lunch, but not close enough to supper yet.

"Of course not. Why would you ask such a silly thing?"

"Well, correct me if I'm wrong, but I saw some looks between you and Cam. Heated, intense looks. What did you do this weekend while the boys were away?"

Serenity couldn't stop her cheeks from blooming a light shade of red. And damn it, she couldn't blame it on the cold since they'd been inside long enough for her to warm up by now.

"We might've hung out together. At his house."

"Hmm-mmm. More details, please."

Hope said it so innocently, even though the glee in her eyes said she wanted every dirty morsel. Serenity laughed so hard, she snorted.

"He built me a sleigh. A huge, beautiful sleigh."

"Please tell me you had sex in said sleigh. Because the way your eyes lit up when you said sleigh said you better have."

They giggled together, Serenity covering her mouth when she thought she was getting too loud. The last thing she needed was one of them, especially her boys, to come investigate why they were laughing so hard.

"Maybe. You should see it. The intricate details. The amount of work he had to put into it. I can't believe he made that for me."

"I can." Hope's brows rose in disbelief. "That man has had it bad for you for the longest time. I'm glad you finally see it."

Serenity set down the butterknife she was using and let out a deep breath. "I'm scared, Hope. I'm going to screw it up somehow."

"Yeah, I felt like that too, with Mase. I made everything so hard for him. That's what love does to you. You've been burned once by your douche ex. It's okay to be cautious, even if I know Cam's a good guy. You're doing the right thing. I didn't mean to make it seem like you should've jumped at a chance with him sooner. I'm just saying I'm glad you two are together now. He deserves happiness as much as you do."

She smiled, yet didn't know how to respond to that.

Were they together?

Was it official?

They hadn't exactly talked about it. Not that they had much of a chance yet.

"I need to see this sleigh. Where is it?"

"At his house still."

That was another thing they needed to talk about. She hurt his feelings when she said she didn't want it at her house, and she needed to rectify that. It was a beautiful piece and it deserved to be shown off. Though it was also special.

She didn't know what the hell she wanted. Other than she wanted Cam in her life.

Because Hope was right. She was scared because she loved him. She could see that clearly now. Love made everything a hundred times more frightening than it should be.

10

CAM WAVED to a few people as he walked down the street from the hardware store, carrying a bag of supplies in his other hand. As long as he kept his eyes on the prize—his truck—he wouldn't be stopped and forced to chat with anyone. Not that he wouldn't if someone got the jump on him, but he preferred not to.

It had been a long week. A very long and trying week. Five days of not seeing Serenity. Sure, they texted and talked a few times on the phone, but nothing face-to-face. She had said she was swamped with work, which he didn't think she was lying about. Why would she? Plus, she worked the night shift at the diner three nights this week. She had even picked up the shift tonight for Tara, despite saying they'd hang out together. When she texted the news, he tried not to take it personal. It was a Friday night, and Tara was down a server. Serenity was the type of person who helped out a friend. She was also a single mom, so he imagined any extra cash was always a good thing.

So, no, he didn't take it personal—much.

They had to talk about them. What they were, what the previous weekend meant. They had sex. Was that all it was? Since Sunday, leaving without a kiss good-bye. Even with the boys telling him he could kiss their mom in front of them, he left without doing so. She didn't know they had the conversation, and she might not be comfortable with it. So he left with a smile and a small hole in his heart. Like something precious between them was slipping away and he didn't know how to bridge that gap. He didn't even know how it was created. Hell, it felt like it'd been there since the moment they met. The question remained, how did he fix that bridge? How did he get to the other side safely?

Hopefully, even though they had two parties to wrangle, they'd have a moment to themselves to chat. Perhaps after the family party and he dropped them off at home. He hadn't said anything yet, but he wanted to drive. He wanted that opportunity to get an invite in after the party.

Sure, the conversation could wait, but he didn't want to wait much longer. It was weighing heavy on him.

"Hey, Cam."

The safety of his truck was only a few feet away and he hadn't made it. Cam turned around and met Stephen's stoic gaze. He was dressed in his uniform, so on duty. They never stopped and chatted anymore. Even two weeks ago when Serenity had the incident with Sherry, Stephen didn't stick around to talk. So why now?

"Hi."

He didn't have anything to say to him. If Stephen had something on his mind, then he could spit it out, but Cam wasn't going to give him more than anything but the bare minimum.

"How's Serenity?"

"Fine."

Stephen shifted on his feet, his eyes drawing to the ground then back up as if he decided in a split second he shouldn't avert his gaze.

"I have two kids of my own. I feel for her. Nobody should be bullied."

No, they shouldn't. But he didn't want to talk to Stephen about this. First, it wasn't any of his damn business. For all Cam knew, this was his way of garnering some information out of him so he could gossip. Second, why was he speaking to him about it like Royce and Randall were his kids? They weren't. Even if he saw them that way at times. He'd love nothing more than to take over that role. He loved those boys so damn much.

"I'm sorry."

Cam's brows drew low. "For?"

Stephen swallowed hard. "For the shit that went down with Melanie."

"Look, man, I don't have time for this. I don't want to go down memory lane."

"I wanted to say I'm sorry. I wish we were still friends."

Cam shrugged. "Yeah, well, you dumped that friendship how many years ago when you picked their side over mine. I don't need that kind of friendship in my life. I gotta go."

He didn't stick around to see what else Stephen had to say. The entire encounter was odd. Why now, after so long, did he want to apologize? It made no sense. Cam didn't have the energy to focus on it anyway. He had too many things to worry about. Like Serenity and how she was doing. If they were good. They were venturing into a new territory that scared him and exhilarated him at the same time.

The rest of his day went by in a blur. When he got home,

he showered, made supper, and ate with his phone in another room. The last thing he wanted to do was constantly look at it for a text from Serenity. That would be dumb. She was working. She didn't have time to text him, and about what? How much she missed him? Because damn, he missed her like crazy. Going an entire week without seeing her was too much.

He slept horribly, tossing and turning the entire night. After having two cups of coffee and his phone remaining silent for the longest time in the history of having the dumb device, he finally gave up.

He called her.

She answered on the second ring, sounding groggy and telling him he had woken her up. It was only nine o'clock. Not too early, but not terribly late.

"Shit, I'm sorry. I didn't mean to wake you up."

"It's okay. I should get up. It's going to be a busy day, and I can't lay around in bed for most of it. I didn't get home until really late. It was an insane night."

"What do you need done and I'll do it. Relax. You need it." Especially with being on her feet all night long, serving people, rushing to and from the kitchen. Working at the diner wasn't easy. Not that everyone was rude and insistent about how their meal was prepared, but Cam knew some customers didn't give a shit. He knew she dealt with a few leeches here and there.

"You're too good to me, you know that?"

He didn't see it that way, but it was nice to hear it anyway. "What time do you want me there? What can I do to help?"

"We can meet you—"

"I'm driving, Serenity. Let me do this. Please."

He didn't want it to turn into an argument, but he had to put his foot down on this. It was all part of his plan for the evening, and he couldn't have her ruining it.

"I still have to make a seafood salad for my parents' house and wrap a bajillion presents. How are your wrapping skills?"

They sucked.

"Not too bad."

"I'll start a pot of coffee. No waffles this time."

So he was invited over already. He'd take it. Because seeing her was the only thing he had wanted all week long.

"I'll bring donuts. Make it even easier for you."

There was a moment of silence from her.

"So, so good to me. Hurry your butt up. I love the kind with chocolate frosting. And sprinkles. Lots and lots of sprinkles."

"You got it."

And anything else she ever wanted in life.

THE WATER POUNDED on her shoulders, hot and scalding. She never liked lukewarm showers. It had to be hot. So hot, she stepped out with red skin. It soothed her rather than hurt her. Her sister could never understand the reasoning behind it, and Serenity didn't try to explain it. It was just something she enjoyed. After a long night of being on her feet and barely getting any sleep, she needed a nice hot shower to wake her up and get her body going for the day. It was going to be another long one.

This time filled with too much Christmas cheer.

"Mom, Cam's here!" Royce shouted through the bathroom door.

Crap!

"Okay, be right out."

She didn't want to get out, but there was no delaying the inevitable. They had to suffer through two Christmas parties today, and she had to pretend she enjoyed it all.

She dried herself off, dressed, brushed her teeth and combed her hair, walking out of the bathroom feeling better but not fully up to power.

The boys and Cam were in the dining room munching on donuts. The wonderful aroma of coffee filtered into the room, making her senses awaken even more.

"You started a pot of coffee. That was supposed to be my job. I guess I took a longer shower than I meant to."

Cam smiled and leaned forward like he wanted to kiss her good morning, but stopped short before actually doing the deed. It nicked her heart a bit, until she realized they couldn't do any public displays in front of the boys until she had a chat with them. To see what they thought about her dating Cam.

Was that what they were doing?

That was another thing she needed to do. Have a chat with Cam as well.

"Like I said, I'm here for you. Relax, enjoy your coffee and donuts. Where are the presents I need to wrap?"

"Yeah, we got this covered, Mom." Royce pulled out a chair and waved his hand in front of it with flare. "Relax. The men have it covered."

She saw Randall puff out his chest a bit, and she couldn't help but smile as she took a seat. "If you all insist."

"We do." Randall pushed the box of donuts closer to her. "Two spoonfuls of your coffee creamer, right?"

She nodded.

"Be right back." Randall rushed out of the room.

"I can help a little bit you know."

Cam pointed to the donut with a glob of chocolate frosting and way too many sprinkles that she knew he must've specifically asked for. Maybe even paid extra for it. "Enjoy your breakfast. Where are the presents?"

She wasn't going to win this war, if that's what she wanted to even call it. Having someone else—three someones—do everything for once didn't sound so bad. Her back still hurt and her feet ached, and despite taking some aspirin last night, she had a slight headache lingering in the back of her skull.

"They're in my office in the closet. Each present is labeled to who it belongs. The wrapping paper is sitting in the corner in a red bin."

Despite hating shopping for presents, she managed to get some this week for the party. She had no choice, so there was that. Unfortunately, she still had to shop for the boys and Cam. A few hours of shopping had done her in, and she had caved before she finished it all.

"We're on it." Then Royce left the room.

She and Cam shared a look before he finally dipped in for a short kiss.

"I missed you this week," he whispered, his hand brushing her cheek. Then his thumb caressed her lips and fell to his side.

"I missed you too."

It hadn't been intentional that they hadn't seen each other. A few new clients popped up for her day job, and Tara called asking for help. She was having a difficult time finding a full-time replacement for the server she lost, and Serenity couldn't say no. Not when she heard the desperation in Tara's voice. Not that Tara would ever beg for help, but she heard the quiet plea that she had nowhere else to turn.

Though she missed him, it had been nice to have a break. For time to think about them and where their relationship should go from here.

She had come to the conclusion she was still a bit confused, a bit leery to put herself out there. Eric had damaged her. He had shaken her sense of stability. One minute she thought they were a team, and the next he was dropping her like a hot potato. It would be so much easier if she didn't have two boys who relied on her. If things with Cam didn't work out, it wouldn't just be her who would be crushed; they would be as well. They adored Cam so much, she couldn't bear to see them hurt by his abandonment as they were with their father. Although she had jumped in with both feet last weekend sleeping with him, a whole week apart had let the fear slither in that they shouldn't have slept together.

She knew without a doubt that if she and Cam didn't work out, her heart would be broken far worse than it had when she lost Eric.

Cam straightened when he heard a noise behind him, and two seconds later, Randall walked into the room with her cup of coffee. She took a sip, impressed it tasted like she made it, and smiled in appreciation.

"Perfection, honey. Thank you."

"On to wrapping," Randall said a little too excitedly, as if he and Royce liked doing that sort of thing.

She knew none of them, Cam included, enjoyed wrapping presents. She didn't even enjoy it. It was one of her least favorite things about Christmas, and well, she pretty much hated everything about the holiday.

"Yo, what are you two doing? I'm doing this all myself," Royce hollered, appearing back into the room.

Cam chuckled and followed Randall out of the room.

She took another sip of her coffee, inhaling the wonderful scent. Then she grabbed the donut overflowing with chocolate and sprinkles and took a large bite. Oh, the flavors and the texture and the decadence of it all.

Maybe this day wouldn't be so bad after all.

11

SNICKERS FILLED THE ROOM, and Cam resisted the urge to roll his eyes, though he did stick out his tongue at the two rascals helping him wrap presents.

"I thought you told Mom you were good at wrapping presents," Royce said as he pointed at the monstrosity sitting in front of him.

The edges were all crumpled, not folded as neatly as he had hoped, and the mound of tape covering it didn't paint a pretty picture.

"I said I wasn't too bad at it. Not that I was good at it. Not a lie."

"Not a full truth either," Randall said.

"Hey, I wouldn't talk much. You two aren't that much better." Cam's brows rose as he eyed both of their lopsided wrapping going on.

"What did you get Mom, Cam?" Royce asked as if it were an innocent question.

Well, it was, except for the fact he had already given Serenity her present and she didn't seem to like it. Sure, they had sex in it, something he would always cherish, but the fact she wanted to hide it from the world hurt.

Of course, he had to remember—thanks to the boys— she didn't like Christmas for some reason. He hadn't known that when he built it, but it would've been nice to know. He worked hard on that sleigh. Put a lot of sweat and tears into it. Okay, he might've not actually cried when he cut himself, but he had a few too many nicks and bruises from it.

"He got me a beautiful sleigh."

Cam whipped around to see Serenity standing in the doorway. She looked adorable holding her coffee cup with her hair damp and her eyes looking refreshed and relaxed for the first time since he arrived.

She walked into the room and sat in the chair in the corner.

"He built it, actually. The craftsmanship still astounds me. The amount of work you put into it. It's so beautiful, I'm still speechless."

Okay, so maybe he misinterpreted everything. She liked it. But then why did she want to hide it away from everyone?

"That is so cool. We want to see it," Royce said, barely looking at Randall, who nodded his head in full agreement.

"Why didn't you bring it home, Mom?" Randall asked.

Yeah, explain the reasoning again. Cam would love to hear it.

"Well, it's very big. Like Santa should be using it for Christmas Eve to deliver all his presents." Her eyes rounded in disbelief and she chuckled. "I don't know where to put it. And I don't want everyone in the neighborhood thinking they can sit in it and try it out or something."

She had said that to him as well, and he had thought it an excuse. But hearing it again, it made sense. He didn't want that either. He didn't make it for everyone in town. He made it for Serenity.

"I'm not sure how Cam would get it here either."

A mangled laugh escaped before he could stop it. "My truck and a trailer."

His eyes connected with hers, and he knew she saw the hurt. He hadn't meant for it to slip out. Today was supposed to be a good day with no bad vibes anywhere. At least not until this evening when they got home and he planned to have the dreaded chat about them.

"Right. Of course. Silly me." Then she stood up. "I should do my hair and stuff. Unless you boys need help."

Her eyes trailed to the wrapped presents, though she didn't say anything about the state of wrapping. The laughter in her eyes told him what she thought of their skills. He appreciated the fact she didn't verbally point it out.

"We got this." He smiled, trying to dispel the negative energy he felt rising and swirling around the room.

She nodded and left.

"A sleigh, uh?" Royce chuckled. "I bet it looks awesome."

"I'm pretty proud of it. I wish I would've known she didn't like Christmas as much as I thought."

"Oh, she likes the sleigh. You could hear it in her voice. Mom thinks she hides things well, but we can decipher her tones. That was her expressing joy about it." Randall frowned. "She's right about the neighborhood. People would help themselves sitting in it without asking. They do it all the time during Halloween when she puts the creepy throne chair in the yard."

Cam loved that chair. She found it at some craft fair a few years ago. The wood was shaped like bones and crafted into a throne-like chair with skulls at the end of the armrests. People loved to stop and take pictures sitting in it. He even had one sitting in it.

They were right. He remembered her expressing her irritation that people, even ones she didn't know, would stop and sit in it without asking her permission. Though she never said anything to the people. No one ever did anything else on her property or made a mess. It was for fun, so she let it slide.

She was right. The sleigh was special, especially since they had sex in it. Like she had said, christened it in a way. He didn't want random people sitting in it.

But where did he put it? How did she enjoy it without people overstepping their boundaries and trying to enjoy it too?

"You and her will figure something out. I know you will." Royce said it so confidently, it frightened Cam.

These boys seemed to have high expectations of something happening between him and their mom. He didn't want to disappoint them. Were they as honest with her as they were with him about them getting together?

The conversation moved on, and soon all the presents were wrapped. They packed everything up, separating them into bags for the first party and some for the second party. After helping Serenity finish getting a few other tasks done, they were ready to leave for Hope and Mase's party.

They were one of the first to arrive. Christmas music was being played in the background. The house was filled with wonderful scents from all the goodies baked and food laid out on the table.

Elliot and Lynn were there with their two kids, Laura and Eloise, and Royce and Randall flocked to Laura. More like Randall did as if they were good friends. Royce hung back, quieter than he usually was. Randall was always the shy one, Royce the outspoken one. But here, the roles were reversed.

Cam tried to keep his smile in as he watched them interact. If he wasn't mistaken, Royce had a crush on Laura. Aww, to be young again.

Then his eyes found Serenity chatting with Lynn and Chasity, Hope's sister. His heart pitter-pattered as if he were in Royce's shoes talking to Laura. Like a giddy teenager hoping his crush liked him as much as he liked her. But in his case, he hoped she loved him as much as he loved her.

"I haven't seen you in a while. How's everything going?" Elliot asked, taking a sip of the eggnog drink he had picked up from the buffet table.

Cam had grabbed one himself. It was good, and he generally didn't enjoy eggnog much.

He answered with what one usually did, a simple 'life's good,' even though he had too much turmoil going on inside him. The afternoon passed in a blur. Good talks, laughter, and great food. Not even Marybeth stopping to chat with him had brought the mood down.

"I hear you made Serenity a sleigh. When do we get to see it?"

Never.

Cam shrugged. "I'm not sure. How's everything with you?"

Easiest way to deflect a conversation with Marybeth was to switch all the attention to her. Because Marybeth loved nothing more than all the attention. Her wide, brilliant smile said she was more than happy to oblige his question. He knew the only reason Marybeth had been invited was because her father worked for the city council. With Hope being the new mayor-elect, she invited everyone she'd be working with soon. Nobody wanted

Marybeth here, but boy could they all pretend it didn't bother them.

When it was time to leave, the sadness hit Cam harder than he thought it would.

If he wasn't mistaken, Serenity looked a bit apprehensive to leave as well. Though the boys looked excited to go and see family.

Royce hardly said a word to Laura, and Randall was animated in his good-bye.

The ride to her parents' house was filled with loudness, the boys' excitement filling the space. Because the sun was setting, the area getting dark, Cam thought it'd be okay to reach across the seat and grab her hand. He could sense her nerves.

They didn't look at each other, but she squeezed it as if saying thanks.

After that, the rest of the night didn't seem so scary.

They could do this. Together.

THIS WAS GOING to be the worst night ever. Serenity knew it. Sensed something foreboding just waiting to happen. Sure, the party at Mase's and Hope's house was enjoyable. Great food, smooth drinks, wonderful conversation. But she knew she'd have a good time there. It was her friends, and she never had a problem with her friends.

Family was a whole different story.

She appreciated that Cam recognized her anxiety. His comfort in the truck helped to alleviate some of her nerves. Nothing would erase all of them, but having a few vanish was better than nothing.

When they pulled into her parents' driveway and saw

the few cars already in attendance, she knew she'd get an earful from her mother for being *late*. Of course, she wasn't late. It was a little after four thirty, and her mother told her to be there by five, and the party didn't start until six. So all these cars meant everyone else was simply way too early. Not her fault. If anything, she was early, too, for her appointed time. It wouldn't make a difference. Her mother would fuss about it. Because if everything wasn't perfect, it was a tragedy. Same thing every year, just a different house and a different sibling. Her mother and all her siblings were the same. All the cousins handed the baton over to the next. She hated that this year was her and Opal's turn. Not that Opal let it bother her. She rarely let anything bother her. It was so nauseating.

"Yes, Uncle Tuck is here." Then Royce and Randall were flying out of the vehicle, barely closing the doors, their excitement was so off the charts.

"He duels them in a racing game every year. My boys will be glued to the gaming system all night."

Cam squeezed her hand. "That doesn't sound like a bad thing." Then he leaned forward and kissed her, brushing his warm hand against her cheek. "You okay? If it's too much I'm here, I can leave."

Her grip on him tightened. The last thing she wanted was for him to leave. "It's not you. This party gives me anxiety every year. I'm glad you're with me. Now kiss me again because it helped to calm me down."

This time the kiss was longer and deeper. His tongue dipping in, exploring, and igniting senses that had been burning on low all week long. How had she not seen him all week? It hadn't been intentional. Work had slammed her, and all week she'd been so tired. Even cooking supper had drained her. Laundry was piled up. The house needed to be cleaned. She did nothing because even the thought of doing any of it exhausted her.

"Okay, we should go in before my mom starts a search party," Serenity whispered against his lips, chuckling. Half-joking, but honestly, half-serious because her mother could be like that. She was like a drill sergeant when it came time to host the Christmas party. To think it had never always been like this.

"Don't let my mother intimidate you. She bosses everyone around."

"It's all good. I can handle it."

As soon as they walked into the warm house, her mother nipping at her heels, the shocked expression on Cam's face said he regretted his last words. That he wouldn't be able to handle this. Her mother immediately ordered him to put the presents around the tree. But not just pulling them out of the bag and laying them anywhere. They had a designated spot and were to be put down in a precise manner. He looked frightened, like he'd mess it up, but always one to go with the flow and not back down from a challenge, he nodded and marched to her tune.

She was forced to follow her mother to the kitchen to put the seafood salad in the fridge and dropped off the ornaments in the living room in the corner. Her mother didn't even stop in her spiel of instructions to get a proper introduction with Cam.

"Hey, you," Opal said, bumping her hip with hers as she peeled potatoes. "Cam's looking yummy in that red sweater. You all should've worn matching sweaters like a cute little family."

She snorted, shaking her head at her sister's ridiculousness. They weren't a family. Though, as the day wore on, the idea didn't bother her. Not like the reservations that had plagued her this morning. Cam was in her life so much—not technically a boyfriend—that he did feel like part of the family. Maybe it wouldn't be so bad if he inserted himself even more. Yet it still frightened her. What happened if they grew apart? How would her boys feel? How would she ever trust a man again? Was it worth it to put her heart on the line again? To give her boys hope?

"Ugh. Stop overthinking it. I hate it when you do that."

"Whatever," Serenity said, rolling her eyes. "I'm not doing that."

Opal mimicked her by rolling her eyes, grabbing the broccoli and cauliflower that Mom wanted her to cut up and arrange prettily on a platter. "You are, and you can't hide it from me. Mom seems to like him."

"Mom barely said hello, ordering him around like she's known him her whole life." Serenity made sure to whisper, embarrassed by her mother's behavior, although not wanting her mother to hear. She could've at least smiled, taken a breath, and welcomed Cam into their home with some warmth in her tone.

"Exactly. Mom doesn't just let anyone help with the party. Why do you think Aunt Carly is sitting in the dining room already sipping on a glass of wine? Because Mom knows she'll screw stuff up, most likely on purpose, and she's not happy she arrived so early."

That was very true. But still. She could've been a bit friendlier. Cam was an important part of her life. She wanted to make a good impression with him, and it didn't seem to be going well so far.

"Plus, Cam adores you, so you know those presents will be perfectly placed because he won't want to disappoint."

A slow smile grew. Another true point.

"Anyway, enough about that. Who did you bring to the

party?" Serenity could play the game as well as Opal. Of course, she was a little late to it, but better late than never.

"Nobody. I'm done with men."

"Ugh, now who's the lame one."

"Shut up." Opal threw a piece of broccoli at her.

Serenity's eyes widened, then she picked up a small piece of potato and threw one back. So started the mini food fight until their mom walked in.

"Are you two serious right now? Absolutely not."

That harsh tone and severe frown had them both pausing in midair.

"What do you think about Cam, Mom?" Opal asked so casually as if pondering about the weather as she picked up her pieces of tiny vegetables littered on the counter.

"Oh, he's a dear. I like him."

Seriously? Her mother didn't say much to him. But, like usual, her sister was right. Somewhere between the front door opening and him venturing to the living room, her mom had decided he was a winner.

"Now knock it off and finish up. We have so much to do before everyone gets here."

Off their mother went to another part of the house to do God knew what. The house was filled with holiday cheer, like a Christmas store had puked in it. Christmas music was playing in the background. The fireplace was glowing with warmth. The tree lit up in all its glory. All that had to be done was the food, and that was nearly completed. Her mother worried needlessly. It was another reason she hated this party so much, no matter who hosted it. The anxiety that came with it. It wasn't necessary. When her grandma was alive—

"Ouch, damn it." She dropped the knife, shoving her finger in her mouth as soon as the blood appeared.

That's what she got for letting her mind wander into territory she shouldn't. So stupid of her!

"Eww. Get out of here and take care of that before Mom sees. She'll freak out if she thinks she lost one tiny piece of those potatoes."

Despite how true that was, Serenity laughed, half-snorting. "Thanks, sis, for your concern. It's only a little cut."

"You're fine. You're not bleeding to death. Now get out of here. You owe me big. If she finds out I threw the potato away, I'll be on the shit list, not you."

She left the kitchen with laughter trailing her and dipped into the bathroom before anyone saw. Her finger stung when the water hit it, yet a sigh of relief escaped because it didn't appear too deep. A surface graze. Just like she had said. A little cut.

A knock on the door had her hitting her head on the bottom of the cupboard searching for a band-aid. Damn, that hurt. But not as bad as her finger throbbed. Why could such a little cut make her hurt like she had sliced it right off?

"Serenity? You okay?"

Cam. The only person she needed right now. It was nice to know he wanted to check on her. She knew she wasn't hiding her anxiety as well as she should be.

She opened the door and ushered him in. "Nothing serious. I cut my finger, but it's not that bad. I'm looking for a band-aid. Don't tell my mom." Then she crouched back down in front of the cupboard and continued her search.

"If it's not that bad, why can't you tell your mom? You're sure it doesn't require stitches or something. Let me see."

"It's not that deep. I promise. It's too hard to explain. My mom goes insane about this party. It's better to keep it to myself." She looked up at him, pleading with her eyes for him to understand. "Trust me."

They held the gaze an extra beat before she continued, crying triumphantly when she found the box she was looking for. She nearly bumped her head again, thankful she didn't because that was throbbing along with her finger.

"I have all the presents displayed to the T like your mother asked. I even got a kiss on the cheek for my efforts."

She paused unwrapping the band-aid with one hand and her teeth, as she had her other hand clenched with a wad of toilet paper. Wow. Her mother did like him. She didn't bestow anyone with that kind of treatment, especially people she just met. Despite Cam being in her life for the past year, he had never crossed paths with anyone else in her family but Opal.

"Thanks for being such a trooper. My mom can get crazy with this night. It's only beginning you know."

"Is this one of the reasons you hate Christmas so much?"

What?

Why would he say such a thing?

How did he figure it out?

"What are you talking about?"

"I—"

"Knock, knock in there," her mother's voice crooned from the other side. "I know you two lovebirds can't help yourself, but we still have a few other things to do before everyone arrives. Chop, chop."

Lovebirds?

Her entire family would think Cam was her boyfriend. Of course, she knew that would happen before she even asked him to come. Now that it was officially said, it didn't panic her as much as she thought it would. Shouldn't she be panicking? She should be. Lots and lots of panicking.

Like him knowing the truth about her feelings concerning Christmas. Panic was in full swing about that.

How had he figured it out?

Unfortunately, she'd have to wait to find out.

Disgusting Christmas cheer had to commence.

CAM FOUND himself situated on the couch in the basement with the boys who were playing video games with their Uncle Tuck like they had wanted. As soon as he and Serenity exited the bathroom, she was pulled back into the kitchen and he was given a glass of eggnog—which wasn't as tasty as the one at Mase's—and told to relax by her mother. He feared arguing, so he followed orders without complaint. He could feel the anxiety coming off Serenity in strong waves, and he didn't want to upset her in any way.

Of course, like an idiot, he almost had. The way her eyes rounded at his dumb question that he knew he shouldn't have brought up. It had popped out before he could stop himself.

He sat there stewing on the burning question, though hiding his anxiety about it while the boys had fun. Soon, the house was filling up with people he didn't know, yet they made it easy to fit right in. Serenity had a large family. Lots of aunts and uncles who had several kids of their own. Some who even had kids as well. The house was loud and cheerful.

When he finally reconnected with Serenity, instead of seeing joy and peace on her face like most everyone else, he saw uneasiness in its place.

"Will I be put in the doghouse if I say I enjoyed the eggnog a lot more at Mase's?" he whispered in her ear, dropping a kiss on her neck because he couldn't resist.

Hoping against hope, but also worried he had sent her

mood further down into the rabbit hole, a smile brightened her face.

"No, because I'd have to join you then. My mom can never get it right. No one ever says anything, and shockingly, it's always gone by the end of the night." Her eyes swooped to the nearly empty glass in his hand. "See, you're being such a trooper drinking it."

"Hey, I'm trying to impress everyone here, not get kicked out." His grin inched up a notch. "I'll be grabbing a beer after this, though. Only one. After that, I'll stop. You enjoy yourself tonight. I'm driving. I don't mind."

"I'm not in the mood." She placed her hand on his chest as if hoping that would silence him. Honestly, the expression on her face was enough to keep him quiet. "We'll chat later about stuff. I promise."

"As long as you're happy, I'm happy." Then he snatched a kiss before anyone saw.

The oohs and ahhs behind him said he failed miserably at it.

"Look at these two. How adorable."

"When's the wedding?"

"They have to move in together first."

"Are you pregnant, Serenity?"

"Why haven't we met this yummy man before?"

"He owns his own company. You know I've been wanting a new kitchen. Do I get a discount?"

The last question had Serenity standing taller and hushing her family to stop barraging them with everything on their mind. Cam was a little shocked everyone in the room kept spouting one thing after another.

"A little respect, please. You'd think I'd never brought a man around here before. Honestly, you all should know better."

Her Aunt Candace smiled and shook her head. "You never have, Serenity. This is the first time we've met someone since you divorced Eric."

"Well," Serenity sputtered, "you should still all know better. Think about Royce and Randall, if anything. Maybe we haven't said anything to them."

"So you are getting married?" Uncle Mark asked again.

"No, we're not."

Cam hoped his flinch wasn't as noticeable as it felt. Because the way Serenity said it so forcefully hurt, as if she had punched him with the truth. *We'll never be together forever.*

"Of course, they're not. Not yet, anyway. They'll move in together first," her cousin Moira said as if everyone should know how relationships worked. As if every relationship had the same formula.

"We're not moving in together either. We're not even dating." She paused, stiffening. "Not officially, yet."

So she wanted to make it official? Cam wasn't going to ask that in front of everyone. This entire encounter was embarrassing. The last time he'd been embarrassed to this level was when he found out Melanie was cheating on him. It had been a packed bar with his best friend sitting there refusing to look him in the eye. Then the asshole suddenly found the courage and said things Cam never wanted to hear. That's when Cam had adverted his gaze and walked out. Too bad he couldn't walk out on this moment.

"Well, what are you two waiting for? How does one make it official?" Aunt Carly asked, looking around the room as if someone would have the answer.

He had kind of hoped what happened the previous weekend between them had made it official without saying the actual words. Though he knew that was naive of him.

Serenity wasn't like other women, and having two kids in the picture made it different. He knew they'd have to have a chat about where this thing between them was going, and they hadn't done it yet. He wished they had now.

Serenity stood there like a deer in headlights until someone else spoke up.

"You still didn't answer the burning question we are all wanting to know." Her cousin Mauve, Moira's sister, said, sipping her drink with a coy smile hiding behind it. "When are you due?"

"You're pregnant, Mom?" Royce asked, popping into the room without anyone noticing. Even the aunts, uncles, and cousins sitting around got eerily quiet.

It was all fun and games until the real world popped into the equation.

"No, Royce, I'm not. Mauve was being silly like she likes to be."

He nodded, yet his eyes sought out Cam. "Randall and I wanted to know if you're up for the next race."

Was he ever!

"Yeah, sure." Cam managed a half-grin at Serenity. "You don't mind, do you?"

A simple nod told him enough. She didn't mind he escaped, but she wished she could escape too. There wasn't much he could do to save her from this. He didn't know how to respond to any of it. Based on her responses—and lack thereof—what was between them was what she had said from the beginning.

Sex only.

At least it was nice to know where he stood with her.

He put his game face on and tried to forget everything said in the living room while he played video games with the boys downstairs. When it came time to eat, he stayed out of most of the conversations, though none were as intense as the previous one. Serenity was pretty quiet beside him as well.

After everyone finished eating, it came time to take an ornament and write something they were grateful for that happened throughout the year. Or as Serenity's mom said, "What's one thing that made you so happy you couldn't stop smiling?"

It didn't take long for Cam to write his down.

Finding something I hadn't even been looking for.

He didn't want to make it too obvious because they would read these next year. If by some sad chance he and Serenity weren't speaking any longer, he didn't want her to be embarrassed when it was read out loud. Anybody could've written that and it could mean anything.

But he would always be grateful for meeting Serenity and letting her into his life when he had no intentions of looking for a woman to settle down with. After getting burned by Melanie, being cautious didn't bother him. Better that than getting his heart crushed again.

Of course, wasn't it getting crushed anyway?

Serenity looked at him at the exact moment the thought passed through him as if she heard it out loud.

"What did you write?"

A sly grin formed as he leaned closer. "You'll have to wait until next year."

Her own mischievous grin emerged. "Fine. I won't tell you what I wrote either."

"Fine."

Excited clapping sounded from across the room. "Okay, showtime, people. Grab an ornament and replace it with the one you just wrote," Serenity's mom said, waving her arms rapidly for everyone to get in line in front of the tree.

They made it easy not to get the ornaments confused and accidentally taking one from this year. Last year's ornaments had a green ribbon tied on top of it. This year's had a red ribbon.

Cam waited his turn until he was able to take an ornament and hang it up. He resumed his same spot near the fireplace where Serenity sat as well. The boys were closer to the tree, huddled together with their cousins.

"Who wants to go first?" Serenity's mom asked.

"How about Cam? Open that sucker up!" Opal shouted from the couch.

Why him?

Did she know what was written inside his? They all sort of looked alike. Clear ornament with a piece of folded paper inside and a green ribbon to mark it with some color.

A few more cheered him on and he smiled, standing up. He popped the top off and shook out the paper.

The strip fell to the floor.

Serenity grabbed it before he could.

"I'll read it."

Her smile looked real, but it was the sudden terror in her eyes that him resisting the urge to argue.

What did the strip of paper say?

12

_____

THIS WAS a bad idea and she should've never let Opal talk her into asking Cam to come. He wasn't enjoying himself, and it was all her fault. Well, her family too. How dare they embarrass both of them like that! Popping out questions like they had a right to. The entire time she had wanted to slink to the floor and disappear like a puddle of water slipping through the cracks in the wood. And Cam. Silent, probably stewing and dying to let out his rage at her for her family putting him on the spot like that.

Well, she'd save him from any further embarrassment. If this strip of paper had something inappropriate on it, she'd make something else up. He didn't need any more humiliation coming his way.

She unfolded the paper and chuckled. Nothing too crazy.

"I love homemade pizza. Especially when I don't have to make it. Hint. Hint." Serenity chuckled again. "I wonder who wrote that."

Everyone laughed, pointing hysterically at Uncle Mark, who nodded proudly, then bestowed his wife Susanna with a kiss. Mark was a chef and cooked all the time. Although he enjoyed cooking meals at home as well, pizza was one that he didn't favor most of the time. Susanna wasn't that great of a cook. So it was a little joke between them.

Crisis averted. The paper didn't have anything too ridiculous on it, but it sounded better coming out of her mouth rather than Cam's. He had no idea the joke behind it. It wouldn't have been as funny if he had read it.

From there, Carly jumped in wanting to go next. So it went, everyone reading out loud their happy thoughts from the previous year. When it got to her turn, Cam surprised her.

He snatched the strip of paper out of her hand before she could get a peek at it.

"Seems only fair I read Serenity's since she read mine."

The room cheered on his decision, widening the wicked smile on his face.

Okay, fine. If he was going to pretend he wasn't embarrassed then she could too.

Though the ache to tear the piece of paper from his hand was strong.

His eyes were glued to it, his smile not wavering, but his eyes glittered with something she couldn't read very well.

"Sometimes, the unexpected not only surprises you but can make you reevaluate everything."

"Wow. That's deep." Uncle Mark was the first to speak.

Cam looked up from the strip of paper and laughed. "But very true."

"Well, who wrote that?" Aunt Carly spat. "That doesn't sound very happy."

"It is if that something unexpected makes you happy. It's all in the eyes of the beholder. It's for you to interpret in your own way." Serenity smiled at her mom's response, then frowned when Carly jumped in again.

"So you must've written it. What surprised you, dear? Was it the nasty couple that moved in next door? You're ready to retire somewhere else? Like Florida?"

Her mom stood up, slamming her hands on her hips. "You can be so vicious sometimes."

Then the room erupted into chaos. Everyone tried to talk over each other and jumped into the conversation like they had a right to.

Serenity didn't know what was going on, but leaned back and shook her head.

Cam's warm breath on her neck soothed some of her rattled nerves. "I feel like I should apologize. So I'm sorry."

A whisper of a smile touched her lips as she turned her head. "You have nothing to be sorry about. Fair is fair. I read yours."

"But mine didn't cause this." His eyes widened as he peeked a glance at the room, then pressed his lips together as if trying to hold in a bout of laughter.

His expression had Serenity holding in her laughter, but of course, she lost the war first.

"Stop. We shouldn't be laughing," she whispered, grabbing his arm, needing some contact. Because it had been too long. She needed something to reassure her they were okay. That they would be okay. No matter what had been said or happened here tonight.

"We should go soon."

Cam's eyes flashed with surprise, then he nodded. "If that's what you want to do."

"I'm partied out. It's been a long day." She paused. "Of course, I don't mind one more drink at home. With you."

His lips twisted into a sweet grin that had her matching his. "I would love that."

The volume in the room finally calmed and opening presents commenced. More laughter, cheer, and merriment occurred. Thankfully, no more fighting. Once that was completed, people ventured off into different rooms. The main events of the party were officially done. While the kids loved the present aspect of the night, Serenity knew the adults enjoyed the ornament part. Especially when things like that happened. Someone writing something mysterious and everyone wanting to know who wrote it.

They said good-bye, going room to room, making sure they didn't leave anyone out. Serenity knew she'd get an earful if she did. Her mom gave Cam a big hug and insisted he come back for dinner after the new year so they could chat properly. That was a good sign. Her father had already given her his silent approval, so everything was good there. It was always her mother a person had to win over with a little oomph to it.

As soon as they got home, the boys went to the basement to play the newest video game they had received. Serenity told them one more hour and then it was bedtime; otherwise, they'd be glued to the system into the wee hours of the morning. Cam grabbed them both a drink from the kitchen and she found him waiting on the couch. Even if the boys came upstairs for something, she didn't mind. It was time they knew. That she explained Cam was more than a friend.

She sat down next to him, making sure they were thigh to thigh, no space between them.

"I feel like there's a lot to talk about here."

Cam leaned forward and set his beer down. "It does feel

that way. I don't want to overwhelm you, though. It's been a nice day."

I'd hate to ruin it were the words he left out. She could sense them floating between them as if they had been ripped from his thoughts and shouted into the air.

"But we should."

He nodded. "Okay, you start then."

Fine. If that's how he wanted it.

She set her beer on the coffee table as well, twisting her body so her knees rested on his legs.

"Tell me why you asked me about hating Christmas."

Cam froze for a moment. "If I tell you, you can't get mad or anything."

Interesting. Opal had to have said something to him. Her sister never knew when to stay out of people's business.

"Of course. I won't."

He eyed her critically as if weighing whether she was telling the truth. And she was. Sort of. She'd only lay into her sister a little bit, not a lot.

"The boys told me you're not a huge fan of the holiday. I wish I would've known that before I made the sleigh. Now it seems like the world's worst present."

Her boys?

They knew?

But how?

Cam's hand found one of hers, clamping it. "I shouldn't have told you that. Don't be mad at them."

"Mad? I would never."

Her sister was one story. But her boys...never. Not over something like this. She didn't understand how they knew. She was so careful around them.

Her eyes drew down to their laps, liking the way their

hands looked together. Her smaller one fit so well into his large, roughened hand. As if they were made for each other.

How whimsical and ridiculous were her thoughts now?

Instead of focusing on the issue before her, she was veering into a different territory. An even scarier one.

"I was so careful not to let them know. Maybe I was too cheery." She lifted her head. "Is that even possible?"

Cam chuckled and shrugged. "I was fooled." Then his smile dipped. "Why do you hate it?"

"I used to love it. I didn't fake it when they were younger. It's only been the last few years that it grates on my nerves."

"Okay, but why?"

This wasn't the conversation she wanted to have.

"I don't hate the sleigh either. You need to know that. I love it. You put so much heart and soul into it, it's amazing. I meant what I said about people sitting on it and stuff. I don't want that."

Cam nodded. "I believe you. I don't mind keeping it at my house. I should've made it smaller. I realize that now." He hesitated. "You didn't answer my question."

She pulled her hand from his and scooted away, knowing the second she had she had done it purposely. Not only to put distance between them physically but emotionally too.

"I don't want to talk about it."

"That's fine," Cam answered, nodding. "Do you want to talk about us? Or is that too much too?"

"That's a little harsh."

Cam shrugged again. "I don't even know what's going on here, Serenity. What's going on between us? Are we a couple? Was it just sex? Great question asked tonight too. How does one make it official? I guess a whole week of not seeing each other should've been clue enough for me."

"That's not fair and you know it. It was a busy week for me."

Cam sighed. "You're right. That wasn't fair. The question still stands, though."

"My boys—"

Cam held up his hand, stopping her. Because he generally didn't interrupt her, she allowed it. Or maybe she was afraid to keep talking because so far this chat wasn't going in the direction she wanted it to.

"I know they are the most important thing in the world to you. I would never do anything to ruin that. I would never step in like I have a right to. I would never expect you to put me first over them. Any man who would expect that is complete shit." She nodded when he paused, appreciating he understood her feelings on that. She knew he would never expect any of that either. "But I should add that they've already told me that they don't mind if we date. That's kind of when the Christmas conversation popped up. So if you're holding back because of them, you don't have to. Of course, I understand if you want to talk to them first before we make anything official between us."

Wow. Well, that was completely unexpected.

She didn't know what to say or where to begin.

"When....when did this happen?"

"Last weekend. I'm not trying to rush you into anything. No moving in. No marriage." Cam chuckled, which made her chuckle, remembering all the crazy questions thrown their way. "I want to be on the same page with you. I want to be in your life. Last week was one of the longest weeks of my life."

She could attest to the same feelings.

"Cam..."

Of course, she didn't know how to express it. She could

admit he was so much better at sharing his feelings than she was.

"Mom, tell him it's okay and call it good."

They both snapped their attention behind the couch where Royce and Randall stood holding a can of pop and a bag of popcorn.

Royce continued. "We came to ask if it's okay if we eat downstairs. We might've heard part of the convo. We know you don't like Christmas much and we suspect why. We also know you and Cam should stop hiding how you feel. It's cool. We like him. We like seeing you happy."

Still speechless. Her boys knew a lot more than she gave them credit for.

"Yes, you can eat downstairs."

"And you and Cam are a thing?" Randall asked, surprising her once more. Royce was usually the voice for both of them.

It helped her heart that had started racing when they popped into the room to calm some. Knowing that they truly didn't mind was very good to know. The last thing she would ever do was hurt her boys in any way.

She looked at them for the longest time, then glanced at Cam, who looked a lot more relaxed than she felt.

"Yes, we are." She tore her eyes from Cam before she started crying for some inexplicable reason and nodded at her boys. "Clearly, I'm not as good at hiding things from you two as I thought. I don't hate Christmas." Despite using that word previously.

"Mom, it's okay. You don't have to pretend with us. We get it." The sadness in Royce's eyes told her that he did understand her adversity to the wretched holiday. She didn't talk about it much with them, and maybe that had been a mistake on her part. "So, yeah. You two have fun, and we won't make a mess. Promise!"

Then her boys were exiting the room and silence reigned.

She took her time meeting Cam's gaze.

"If I tell you why I hate Christmas, we'll need another drink or two."

"I shouldn't have more than one."

Her butt scooted closer, then she grabbed both of his hands this time. "Unless you don't drive tonight. Then it doesn't matter how many you have."

"Are you asking me to spend the night?"

Her boys gave her the all-clear with Cam. They seemed to love him. Why not jump right into the relationship with both feet? She wanted this to work between them.

"I am."

Cam leaned forward and answered her with a delicious kiss that told her she should lock her bedroom door tonight so no unexpected visitors popped in.

HE DIDN'T WANT to rush this—whatever was happening between them. Shock was still reverberating around him that she had asked him to spend the night. With the boys in the house.

She pulled away first, and he didn't argue. Why should he? They had all night together now. She grabbed both bottles of beer and handed him one. Then clinked his.

"To ending on a good note."

"That's definitely something to cheer." And it also meant he shouldn't bring up the hatred for Christmas, despite her saying she'd tell him. Would that mean they'd still end on a good note?

"Let's get the other conversation out of the way." Serenity took a huge gulp of the beer, averting her gaze.

"Hey." He brushed her cheek, smiling when she looked at him. "Not if it's going to upset you. You don't have to."

"I want to. Some might think it's silly, and you know, I think half of my family would if they knew." A lame chuckle escaped. "Who am I kidding? They do know. My boys figured it out, so obviously I don't hide it as well as I thought."

"You fooled me."

Even offering a goofy grin did nothing to erase the sadness on her face.

"My grandma passed on Christmas Eve. Eight years ago. She went to lie down for a rest, and I'm the one who went to wake her up to give her an hour warning the party would be starting. It was the worst Christmas Eve ever."

"Oh, Serenity..." He had no idea what to say.

That was heartbreaking. Knowing that, it wasn't hard to understand why she hated the holiday so much. He knew she was close with her family. Though she didn't talk about her grandma too much—no doubt painful for her—he suspected she had been very close with her.

He didn't understand why her family would think it's silly, though. That had to have been hard on everyone. Perhaps they hid their pain as well as she hid hers. He had been clueless she hated the holiday.

"After that year, we started having the party a few weeks before Christmas. Maybe people worried someone else would die on the holiday. They all seemed to bounce back from it. Still cheerful. Still being merry. I fake it because I don't want to be the one bringing the party down. I should've known my boys would figure it out. They were only five at the time. So young to understand what had happened. I mean, they knew what happened, but..." She shook her head. "I miss her so much. I know she died peacefully. No pain. But yeah, I don't particularly care for the holiday anymore. That kind of sucked all the joy out of it. My mind always veers to that moment instead of all the happy memories. And I had so many happy memories with her."

He reached out and took her hand. "I can understand why you don't enjoy the holiday. That had to be so hard. I'm here if you ever want to talk. Vent your frustrations." He paused, not sure he was saying the right things. She was still frowning, but it wasn't turning more severe so that had to be a plus. "Share happy memories, if you want. Or not talk about it at all."

"I love how you know the right thing to say."

He laughed. "Really? Because I feel like I never have the right thing to say."

"You do. Trust me." Then she leaned forward and kissed him.

It was a brief kiss, but enough for the moment. Not that he had even expected the tiny kiss because what she laid down at his feet was a lot to take in.

"Now you know a little reason why my mom is crazy about the holiday too. I suspect she wants everything to be perfect because that one year it wasn't. There. Now that's out of the way."

He frowned, yet said nothing. Words still failed him. He didn't want to say the wrong thing. But hell, he didn't know what the right thing to say was either. Her reasoning made sense about her mother, but to rush all that out and then drop the conversation...was he even supposed to respond?

"Do you want to watch a movie or something?"

His gaze flickered to the TV and back at her.

Before he could respond, she jumped in. "Don't worry. I'm okay, Cam. I don't want to dwell on that topic. Now you know why I don't particularly care for the holiday. Let's move on."

He nodded, then held up a finger. "One question." He wasn't even sure he should ask it, but if they were going all in with a relationship, he had to.

"Okay." Though the simple word came out hesitantly.

"What do you do to celebrate Christmas Eve and Christmas Day? I normally go to my parents on Christmas Day, and I'd love for you and the boys to come with, but if it's too much then—"

"I'd love to. The boys would love to. I know they would." Her hand brushed his cheek. "Don't treat me like I'm fragile about the holiday now that you know. It's fine."

But was it? Because it didn't feel fine. She had a lot of pent-up emotions—rightly so—that he felt she hadn't dealt with yet. Of course, it wasn't his place to force the issue, so he'd let it go. Just like she asked. He'd move on. But it didn't mean he'd forget it.

He still didn't want to say the wrong thing, so instead of words, he used his lips to speak. A tender kiss that said, "Okay, we'll move on." Of course, he wasn't sure how he felt about having sex while the boys were home. Even if they did lock the door. That felt weird. Kisses here and there wouldn't hurt. Sleeping next to each other was fine. But doing the actual deed? That felt awkward.

They put on an action movie, one he considered a Christmas movie, though she swore it wasn't. They agreed to disagree. Thirty minutes left to the movie, the boys popped in to say good night. When the credits hit, they decided to hit the hay as well. After getting ready for bed, Serenity closed the door, but she didn't lock it like she had teased. He didn't comment on it because he didn't feel it was necessary to lock it anyway.

He pulled her into his arms, loving how perfectly her body fit next to his.

"Thanks for a wonderful day." He placed a light kiss on her nose, before diving in for a deep, thorough kiss.

Her arms wrapped around him tighter, her legs clinging around his waist, making him harder than he wanted to be. The way her body molded to his. The way her breathing became heavier by the moment. The way the room felt electrified with sexual energy.

"We shouldn't with the boys in the house," he whispered against her lips, their tongues dueling in a gentle battle.

"They won't come in here. They aren't dumb, Cam." Her hands trailed down his back, scooped underneath his boxers, and clamped onto his ass, pushing him into her body even more. "I can be quiet if you can."

It still felt odd to have sex with them in the house. He knew they were old enough to figure out what went on between couples. Some of the movies they had watched were clue enough, though he knew Serenity had talked with them because she had relayed the story to him. It had been hilarious and embarrassing at the same time listening to it. He was so glad he wasn't the one who had to do it. Poor Serenity that she had to when it should've been up to their father. The deadbeat asshole.

"Cam..." Her hands dug into his ass harder, as if telling him she wasn't going to let him get away.

Screw it. If she was okay with it, then he could be too.

"Condom?" Because he didn't have any in his wallet.

She leaned away, a come-hither grin on her face. "Be

right back." Then she broke from his embrace and darted into the master bathroom that was part of her bedroom and not one she had to walk out into the hallway to get to.

That same devilish grin was on her face when she walked back into the room. Her clothes were gone. Obviously, she got naked in the bathroom. He tossed his shirt and boxers off, matching her attire with ease. She ripped the condom package open, then straddled him, running a smooth hand down his chest.

"I don't know why we waited so long to do this. I have so much fun with you. In and out of the bedroom."

Then she donned the condom onto his hard, thick cock, smiling like she'd been bestowed the best present in the world.

Before she could take the lead, he grabbed her by the hips and flipped her, making her squeal in delight. His lips silenced her before anything else could escape.

"You promised to be quiet," he chided playfully.

"Then don't surprise me like that."

"You had top last time. I want it this time."

God, he loved the sly smiles she kept throwing his way.

"I didn't know we were keeping score, but okay. Have your wicked way with me."

Oh, he planned to.

He entered her with one swift stroke, kissing her as he did because he knew her better than she thought. Only a few times having sex and he knew how loud she could be. The moan that wanted to escape was captured by his mouth. The other ones that wanted to be released stayed quiet as he devoured her lips at the same time he devoured the rest of her body. In and out. Hard then slow. Thrust after thrust. All the while her hands played havoc on his skin, roaming up and down his back, gripping his head and sliding through his hair, pulling gently on the ends. She lit him on fire as much as he could feel her own body flaming with desire.

It felt like an eternity, but it didn't take long before she was moaning deliriously into his mouth as she came, clinging to him as if she never wanted to let go. He had no qualms with that. He planned to keep her forever—if she'd have him.

He followed closely after, planting sweet, tender kisses on her neck as he came down from the high.

"Well, I do have to say this is the best after Christmas party sex I've ever had."

He chuckled, lifting onto his elbow. "You're welcome. Wait until the morning comes. I'll show you some great morning sex too."

"Why wait until morning?" Then she was pulling him in for another kiss.

She was right once again.

Why had they waited so long to do this? Best moments of his life. Just being with her.

13

ONE MORE DAY before the boys had Christmas break, and Serenity felt like she was going to go insane with the amount of things on her to-do list. Of course, it didn't help since she and Cam had decided to make an official go at things he had been over every night. The boys wanted him there. She wanted him there. He wanted to be there. It didn't leave any time for her to get things done in the evenings like she usually did. All she had to do was tell Cam and he'd understand. Yet she never did. She enjoyed the time with him.

She'd rather lounge on the couch with him than shop for Christmas presents anyway. The stores were so over-packed she hated even going to get groceries. Another thing she needed to do as well. The refrigerator was starting to look sparse. Not that anyone had complained, even her boys. They could live off cereal and ramen if she let them.

The nice thing about her work was she could take breaks when she needed to. Today seemed like the best day to get a chunk of her list out of the way. Now that she was spending Christmas at Cam's, she needed to add more presents to her list. He had told her it wasn't necessary, but she couldn't go to his parents' empty-handed. It would look rude.

She stopped at the local store in Mason that sold home-made everything. From things made out of wood to soap to pottery items. She loved the store because everything was from people who lived in town. Local store with items made by local people. It was like a one-stop shop for anyone's needs. It was well-known, so when she arrived, the place was hopping. Serenity managed to get in and out in under an hour, which was pretty good because she could linger in there for a long time looking at everything. She ended up buying a beautiful pottery soap dish that was shaped like an octopus. Its tentacles held the dish up. She paired it with a few soap bars smelling heavenly of lavender. Cam's mom would receive that. He had said his mom liked unique things, and that seemed pretty unique to her. She almost bought one herself, it was so fun to look at it.

She purchased his dad a hand-carved wooden sign that said 'fish until I dish.' It made her chuckle for no reason at all and sold her the instant the laughter came out. It reminded her of the silly saying 'shop until I drop.' But, of course, the fishing one meant catch all the fish and then eat it all up. At least she thought so. What else could it mean? Cam loved fishing, as did his dad and brother. She met his dad once, and he had been all decked out in fishing gear, even with a crazy hat with a fish sticking out of the top. She knew he'd love it—or hoped so anyway.

His brother was the hardest for her. Nothing stuck out to her, and even as she walked out of the store with bags in hand, she worried what she got him was ridiculous. But hey, for a vocal ladies' man, candles were a must. So she bought him a few long-stemmed candles and a candle holder to help him woo his ladies. Hopefully, he got a chuckle out of it and not any offense taken.

Next, she shopped for her boys, buying the latest games she knew they wanted and a few other trinkets and gadgets she knew they'd love. They were the easiest to shop for.

She made it home with everyone taken care of but Cam. What did she get a man that deserved everything and more? How did she compete with the sleigh he had hand-built for her? That had to have taken him forever. It was impossible.

The boys found her sitting at the dining room table staring at her computer searching for ideas.

"How was school?" she asked, popping out of the few browsers she had open. No need for the boys to see how much trouble she was having thinking of a present for Cam. They'd tease her and tell her not to worry so much about it. Even Cam would say the same thing.

So why was she making it such a big deal?

Because she couldn't help herself. He deserved something spectacular, and nothing less would be acceptable.

"Good." Royce plopped his backpack on the table.

Randall shrugged and set his backpack down with a little less energy.

"Everything went okay?"

Meaning nobody was picking on Randall still because she'd go all-out psycho again if she had to.

They both nodded, and considering she knew Royce would tell her the truth, she took it at face value.

"Are you excited about the concert tonight?"

Royce was in orchestra and played the cello. His concert had been at the beginning of the month. Every song had been wonderful, despite each one being a Christmas tune. She loved watching and listening to him play. He was going on his third year and getting so much better at it.

Randall was in choir and loved to sing. Though she swore he held back when singing in a group. But at home, he loved to belt out at random times, and he especially loved singing in the shower. His concert was tonight.

"Yeah, I guess. I don't have any homework. I'm going to go chill in my room."

Then Randall walked out, leaving her wondering if something had happened and they were both keeping it from her.

"Don't worry, Mom. It's nothing. He's nervous about tonight. You know how he gets when singing."

She did. Every concert he'd ever been in since elementary school had put his nerves on high. Her sweet, shy boy didn't like being the center of attention, even if it meant he was in a crowd of people and wasn't solely the center.

"Okay, I won't. Cam's bringing over pizza and we'll all drive together."

"Cool. I don't have any homework either. I'm going to go play some games."

Then Royce was bouncing out of the room and she was alone once again.

She went back to her task, slamming the computer shut when she saw the time. She still had no idea what to get Cam, and Christmas was less than a week away.

Cam arrived not too long after she put her computer away and freshened up. His kiss calmed down the anxiety that had been steadily building all day. She had no need to fret. He'd love whatever she got him because that's the kind of guy he was. Easygoing and carefree.

"How was your day?"

Such an innocent question, and yet the cringe on her face spoke more volumes than whatever lame response would've come out of her mouth.

"What happened?"

She waved him off. "Nothing. I went Christmas shopping. Not my favorite task."

His eyes displayed his understanding, and she wanted to cry at how much he truly recognized her discomfort with the holiday.

"I hope you didn't buy anything for my parents. I told you not to worry about them."

She smiled. "They are going to love what I got them. The boys were super easy. Your brother I'm not too sure about." She mock winced, but overall, she thought he'd get a chuckle out of it based on how Cam described his brother.

"They'll love whatever you got, but you shouldn't have stressed yourself out about it." He wrapped his arms around her and pulled her closer. "I don't like seeing you upset."

"I'm not upset."

"Stressed then. Whatever you want to call it. Don't worry about me."

It's as if he sensed she was struggling with him the most. Of course, she would continue to have high anxiety about his present until she actually bought something and then gave it to him. He should know better than to think she wouldn't.

"You're proving to be the hardest to buy for."

"I don't need anything."

"That's what everyone says, and they—"

He silenced her with a kiss, and she couldn't be mad about it because his lips always soothed her.

"My gift from you is just that. You. All I wanted was a chance with you and I'm getting it. I don't need or want anything else. I only want to make you happy."

"Stop being so wonderful."

Cam's delicious laughter settled more of her nerves, but

not all of them. No matter what he said, she had to buy him something.

"Come on," she said, slipping out of his arms and grabbing the pizzas he brought over from the side table in the foyer. "Let's eat. I want good seats for the show."

Hopefully, something amazing would pop into her head because she was running out of time.

CAM SAT NEXT TO SERENITY, holding her hand while Royce sat on her other side. He hadn't been sure he should hold her hand and almost let go, but she was the one to tighten the grip. It was one thing for the boys to know and accept them, but publicly announcing they were dating he hadn't been sure about. Only because he wanted to move at her terms, not his. He was so giddy with excitement that she didn't mind telling the world, that he wanted to lift her hand and kiss the back of it. Of course, he didn't do that. Talk about embarrassing. It was ridiculous how much he felt like he was back in high school worrying about what the other kids thought of him.

Randall looked nervous and out of his element as he stood among his classmates singing. He and Serenity were surprised when after one song was completed, he moved from his spot and took center stage in front of the microphone. She even gasped. Royce made no comment other than to smile wider at his brother who had a short solo part.

When he started singing loud and clear to the beginning of *The First Noel*, Cam couldn't have been prouder. He had a wonderful voice. The only thing that made him sad was the fact Eric didn't show up. Cam knew Serenity had invited him. Before they left, she sent him a reminder text, and she had looked at her phone constantly before the show started. Nothing. Nada. Eric chose to ignore her and his boys.

When the song ended, Cam couldn't stop his loud clapping, and he nearly whooped with joy but didn't want to embarrass Randall. Though he wasn't his dad, he felt the pride deep inside as if he were.

The crowd went wild when the last song was sung. Standing ovation for everyone. Cam was sorry he had missed Royce's concert earlier in the month. He had been invited, but he'd been working on a project for a difficult client and couldn't get away. From now on, that would never happen again. He'd never miss anything for either of the boys. He wasn't their real father, but he'd damn well act like one. A better one than their own father did.

The kids filed out of the auditorium backstage while they waited for the room to empty so they could meet the kids outside.

"I had no idea he had a solo." Serenity looked at Royce. "But you did, didn't you?"

Royce wore a sly grin. "He told me not to tell. He wanted to surprise you. Both of you."

"He was amazing. I've heard him sing, but he was really good tonight." Cam reached out and touched Royce's shoulder. "I'm sorry I missed your concert. That won't happen again."

He didn't know why felt compelled to say that, but it had to be said. Royce needed to know how much he cared about him. Not just his mom, but him and Randall too. Cam knew what it meant to date a mom with two boys. They were a package deal, and one he fully accepted with open arms.

"It's all good, Cam. We have a spring concert."

"I'm there, no matter what."

Royce's smile said he believed him. That's all he needed to see.

"Can I go say hi to my friends?" Royce asked Serenity, who nodded, and off he went to a group of boys standing near the exit.

The room was still emptying, and instead of fighting the crowds, they waited in the row they sat in for it to clear some more.

"You don't have to feel bad about missing his concert."

Cam reached for her hand and finally did what he wanted to do all night: kissed the back of it. "But I do. I should've made more of an effort to make it. I'm so proud of Randall tonight. I'm mad I missed feeling the same about Royce."

"You just keep making it harder and harder."

He frowned. "What harder and harder?"

She shook her head, laughing. "Never mind. You're wonderful." Then she pulled on his hand for them to start moving.

He wanted to argue about whatever she was talking about but didn't. Not the time or place for that sort of thing.

"Well, aren't you two cozy?" Warren, Dawson's dad, said, coming up behind them.

Serenity chose to ignore him, and if she wasn't going to comment, then he'd keep his nose out of it too.

"Your boy was out of tune. Better luck next time."

Serenity swiveled around, and though he held her hand, he didn't stop her. The ache to whip her back around and keep walking was strong. But not his place. Not his kids. All Warren was doing was looking for a reaction. That's what bullies did. He was nothing more than an asshole bullying someone who was clearly better than him. Obviously, like father, like son. Dawson's mother was no better. No wonder the kid picked on others. His parents taught him how to do it.

"I see where your son gets his attitude. Like father, like son."

"Hey, it's not my fault you're a homewrecker. Ruining your family and tearing them apart. Those boys need their father. Not that pussy standing next to you."

Cam tensed, a muscle jumping in his cheek as he clenched his jaw hard.

"You left Eric for that piece of shit. It's your fault your son can't handle a little ribbing."

Serenity let go of his hand and stepped closer, shoving her finger at Warren but not quite touching him. "You stay away from my sons. Your son better too. I won't hesitate to speak to the school and have action taken."

Then she turned around and walked away before he could respond. Cam stared a moment too long, then turned himself. Warren's snickering said he thought he won that little battle.

Far from it.

He knew how much of a mama bear Serenity could be. She wouldn't let anyone hurt her boys.

Cam was amazed at how easily a smile filtered back onto her face when Randall appeared, as if she hadn't been insulted and degraded as she had. He wasn't going to ruin the mood, and Randall didn't need to know what happened anyway. They both congratulated him and hugged him. Cam was so proud and made sure he knew that.

When they got home, Serenity brought out cupcakes— purchased from Lynn's bakery, of course—and they celebrated with the sweet treat. After the boys finished, they went off to do their own thing.

He felt the awkwardness the moment the boys left the

room and it surprised him. The way she wouldn't meet his gaze didn't make sense. He helped clear the table and bring the dishes to the kitchen. She started filling the dishwasher, ignoring him. As the end of the night raced through his mind, he realized she hadn't made much eye contact with him since the incident with Warren.

"Are you okay?"

"I'm tired. Long night."

Yet she didn't turn around to speak, to look him in the eye. The dishes clattered loudly as she put them in the device.

"Did I do something wrong, Serenity?"

Because, for the life of him, he couldn't figure out what he could've done to upset her so much.

She stood up, her entire body rigid, and finally turned around. The fire in her eyes matched the thinning of her lips.

"You stood there, Cam. You just stood there and let him speak to you like that. Let him say those terrible things."

"What was I supposed to say? He was looking for a fight."

She threw her hands up in the air. "I don't know. Anything. Something. You never speak up."

He frowned. "What? I have no idea what you're talking about."

"In the salon with Sharon. When we ran into Eric at the theater. At my parents' Christmas party and everyone pelting us with questions. Tonight. You never step in. You never have my back. I can't do this with you if you're not going to be my partner. I won't be the only one trying to hold things together again. It's not fair."

He had to stay calm and not lose his shit. But what she was slinging at him wasn't fair. Though he had to remain calm, he also couldn't *not* respond. "I didn't think it was my place to step in. They aren't my boys. We weren't even dating then for half of those things. I didn't think you'd want anybody, especially some guy, just stepping into your business. I also know you can handle it. You're making it seem like I should've treated you like some damsel in distress when you're far from it."

"Not your boys? Fine, they aren't. But you can't tell Royce you'll never miss one of his concerts and then in the next breath say they aren't yours. Act like they don't even matter."

"Whoa. You know I care about them. I don't know where this is coming from, but if you want to talk about fair, saying that shit isn't fair."

"He called you a pussy and you let him. We are now dating and you didn't stand by my side so you can't use that excuse for this one."

Wow. He was utterly speechless. This was unknown territory for him, and he had no idea the proper response. He'd never dated a woman with kids before. Was he supposed to assume the role of their father, even though they just started dating? He didn't think she'd want him to step in as if he had authority. At least, not until they had a chat about it. It hadn't been in any of the conversations this past week.

"Honestly, Serenity, what did you want me to do or say? Hit the guy? I'm not a violent man. I don't like to give assholes like that the satisfaction of a reaction. You know when I found out Melanie cheated on me with my best friend, he was sitting right there. He had the balls to tell me I didn't appreciate her enough. That I wasn't man enough for her. That I couldn't satisfy her as well as he could. My best friend of fifteen years said that to me. To my face. You know what I did? I stood up and walked out. Because I have nothing to say to someone who has no respect for me. To someone who I thought was my friend, who I thought would always have my back and not disrespect me by sleeping with my girlfriend. People like that are looking for a reaction. Maybe he wanted me to hit him or lash out because he felt guilty. Well, I refused to give him that. I refuse to give that to anyone, including that asshole tonight. While I love those boys of yours as much as I love you, I am not going to assume I should step in unless you talk about those things with me first. Yet instead of telling me it's okay to act like their dad of some sort, you throw accusations at me like I'm the bad guy here. I'm not the bad guy. I can't do this with you if I'm always going to be the bad guy for no reason at all. I'm not Eric. Don't suddenly treat me like I am."

She stared at him for the longest time but said nothing.

He interpreted that as 'you can leave.'

So he did.

14

CAM DIDN'T BOTHER LOOKING up or turning his head to see who knocked on his door. Instead, he took a sip of his beer and continued to stare at the TV in front of him. The couch bounced when his brother plopped down next to him.

"You haven't been returning my calls. Your texts are short, and you don't even answer those all the time either." Vin exhaled slowly. "It reminds me of the time when you found out Melanie cheated on you. Talk to me."

But that was the thing. He didn't want to talk about it. With anyone. Not Mase who had bothered him the past few days. Not his mom who asked him the kind of food Serenity and her boys liked. He couldn't answer that question because, as far as he knew, they wouldn't be joining them for Christmas anymore. Why make food they liked if they wouldn't be eating it? Hell, it was Christmas Eve and he hadn't talked to Serenity since the day he walked out.

He had said good-bye to the boys, not wanting to leave on bad terms with them. But he hadn't spoken to them either in the days since.

It hurt. It all hurt so badly he felt like his heart had been ripped from his chest, crushed and beaten until it was nothing more than a bloody pulp.

Out of nowhere, the beer bottle disappeared from his hand, wrenched away by his brother, who stood up and threw it in the trash. Cam wasn't drunk if that's what Vin thought. It was early afternoon, and despite sitting in his workshop all morning, that was the first beer he had opened. Maybe after a few more he might do something about the dumb sleigh sitting behind him.

Burn it.

Destroy it.

Make sure not a piece of it remained.

Sensing it behind him shattered his heart into a million pieces all over again.

The couch jostled again when his brother resumed his seat.

"You're not doing this again. Retreating into yourself like shit doesn't bother you. Ignoring the issue. It took forever for you to go on another date. Even longer to let another woman in."

A sad excuse for a laugh slipped out. "And look how that turned out."

"So this is about Serenity. What happened? You have to talk to me. I'm not leaving until you do."

This Cam knew. Vin could be like an annoying ant. Appearing and disappearing and then reappearing trying to squash it and never accomplishing the goal. Nasty little buggers.

It still didn't mean he wanted to talk about it. He wanted to stare at the TV and listen to the man drone on about how to build a shed. It didn't even matter he could build a better one. But the sound of the instructions and the hammering, sawing, and loud noise soothed his broken soul.

"Mase doesn't know what happened either. If you can't talk to your best friend, you should at least be able to talk to your brother. You owe me for getting those tickets for you. I had to agree to a date with a woman I've been trying to avoid for two years. I am not happy about that."

Cam finally turned his attention to his brother. "What woman?"

Vin's brows rose in disbelief that was what got his attention. Well, hello. Mister Ladies' Man didn't avoid women. He loved and doted on them like they were his favorite thing in the entire world, which they were.

"You don't know her. You've never met her. But I work with her, and I don't dally with women I work with."

Cam snorted. "Wow, never known you to lie to me before."

Vin rolled his eyes and sighed. "Okay, fine. I don't mess around with nice women. She is a damn sweetheart, and I'm not sleeping with her knowing she'll want more. I don't want more. I like fun. She's Miss Suzy Homemaker. I don't know what she expects out of this date."

"When is this date?"

He wasn't even going to touch the no dating and forever kind of woman topic with his brother. Cam had an inkling the reason his brother didn't do relationships was because of what happened to him. It could never happen to Vin if he didn't allow it to happen. It made him sad that something that happened in his past shaped the way Vin viewed women. Not all women were alike. Cam knew this. He had thought Serenity would be different. And she was. She didn't cheat on him. But she didn't respect him enough to be honest with him. Instead, he was getting blamed and treated for Eric's old habits. Obviously, what he did to her shaped her view of men, no matter how much she thought it didn't.

Of course, Eric seemed like the type to speak up when someone else insulted them.

Hell, Cam didn't know what to think anymore. All he knew was he didn't deserve to be treated like that by her.

Vin shrugged. "After the new year, I guess. I didn't set one yet. I know she won't let me forget it though. So anyway, enough about me. Let's talk about you now."

His eyes drifted back to the TV. It was only fair.

Ha!

That dumb fair word again.

Was life really fair?

Or just a sequence of bad shit happening over and over again, no matter how hard you tried to change things?

"Okay, fine."

Cam told him everything said between them and the incidents Serenity referenced. He didn't feel any better getting it off his chest. Because for a brief moment as he started to speak, he thought he might.

"Wow, that was heavier than I anticipated."

"Oh, so no brilliant advice."

Vin winced. "That's not territory I understand."

"Same. I didn't think she'd want me speaking for her kids."

"She probably doesn't. If you had, she would've gotten mad. Damned if you do, damned if you don't. Something else is bugging her and she's using that as an excuse."

That was a possibility. He could tell she was stressing about Christmas and the presents and making sure everything would be perfect. No matter how many times he told her not to worry, he knew it only increased her anxiety about it all.

"Have you called her?"

Cam shook his head, frowning. "Why would I call her? I'm not the one in the wrong here."

"Yeah, not really. I mean, you could've knocked the dude on his ass for calling you a pussy. I would've."

"You also got suspended more than me in school for using your fists instead of your brain." Cam touched his chin mockingly as if contemplating. "Oh, yeah, I never got suspended because I know better. Punching someone doesn't solve shit."

"All those other times, they insulted the boys, not you. I get why you didn't step in. This last time you should've."

"Not entirely true. Sharon didn't insult me, but she brought me into the conversation telling me not to date Serenity because she cheated. I could've said something then. I didn't."

"Why not?"

Cam sighed, slouching into the couch. "Why should I voice my thoughts to the entire town? It's not any of their damn business what goes on between Serenity and me. They both wanted to start something, and I didn't allow it by ignoring it. Just like Danny when he told me I wasn't man enough for Melanie. He wanted me to react. Nothing happened because I chose to walk away."

"That dude deserved a punch in the face as well."

"You need to stop thinking with your fists, Vin."

"And you need to get off your ass and get Serenity back. She's good for you. I know how much you love her. I don't want to see you fall into another deep black hole because of a woman."

"I don't know what to say to her. I can't apologize because I don't think I did anything wrong."

Vin blew out a breath, his eyes trailing to the mini fridge. "I shouldn't have thrown your beer away. I could go for one."

Cam chuckled.

"At the very least you have to talk to the boys one more time. You can't leave things hanging with her like this. If you're over, you're over. But they deserve a proper good-bye."

That was a problem. He didn't want to say good-bye. To any of them. He didn't want to lose Serenity from his life. Of course, ignoring the issue wasn't doing him any good.

"So you think I was wrong?"

"I didn't say that. I said you should've punched the asshole, but I get why you didn't. For stepping in as if you're their father, oh hell no, that's not your place. Not unless she told you so. And we both know she didn't. I think you both need to talk it out. Not ignore each other."

"It's Christmas Eve. I can't bother her today."

"And what about tomorrow? You still haven't told Mom they aren't coming. She's expecting them and very excited about it."

That's because Cam dreaded having the conversation. But he should break the news to his mom.

"I don't think I can, Vin. It's hard getting rejected over and over by women you thought cared about you. I won't say Serenity loved me, but I thought she cared."

Vin stood up, grabbed two beers from the fridge, and sat down again, handing one to him.

"One beer and then you make a decision. No negotiations."

That's what his brother thought. But if he didn't want to move from this spot—he didn't—then he wouldn't.

———

"IT SMELLS divine in this joint. That's not actually my sister cooking, is it?"

Serenity chuckled at Opal's wonderment and closed the oven door. The turkey wasn't quite done. Another thirty minutes and it'd be ready.

"Leftover turkey is nice to have. I had a craving for it."

"For a whole-ass turkey?" Opal's brows rose skeptically. "For only three of you? Yeah, okay, sis. Whatever you say."

Opal grabbed the open bottle of wine from the counter and poured herself a glass. "We both know you go crazy with cooking and cleaning when you're upset. I bet if I walk around this place, everything will be sparkling like a brand new chandelier."

As much as she wanted to deny it, all of that was true. She got antsy when her nerves were going haywire. Since the moment Cam walked out, she'd been a bundle of nerves. Regretting the things she said. Not stopping him from leaving. Being such a chicken-shit about calling him. She knew they had to talk, but she didn't know how to reach out.

"Talk to Cam yet?"

Serenity glared at her sister.

"What? I thought you might've grown some bravery since we chatted last night. This is ridiculous. You hate cooking turkey. It's the reason you never host Thanksgiving."

Another truth she couldn't deny.

Because she wasn't a fan of baking or cooking. She only cooked out of necessity to feed her boys. Someone had to. She was the only parent around.

Because Eric never kept up his end of the bargain.

But Cam...

Well, Cam wasn't their father, as he pointed out—something she knew. But he treated her boys like they deserved to be treated. Cooked supper at times. Brought pizza over. She didn't have to worry all the time about serving food when Cam was around. They were a team. Tackling things together. Even before they were officially together. He'd been her rock more than she had realized. Not until she had sleepless nights to think over every little thing that ever happened between them.

"He's not Eric, you know."

This glare was worse than the last one she delivered. Of course she knew that. Cam was everything she ever wanted in a man.

That was the problem.

She had made it seem like he was like Eric. He had every right to get upset and leave.

"He let Warren call him a pussy. He stood there and took it."

That she didn't understand. After she thought about it, she was grateful that he didn't overstep his boundaries about the boys. He was right. She wouldn't want just any man she dated to think they had a right to father her boys. But he fell so easily into the role, it felt natural for him to stick up for them. Of course, she had never told him that and so he didn't. She had no problem if he did though. Something she wanted to tell him.

But not sticking up for himself. That made no sense to her. Eric definitely would've given Warren a piece of his mind. Cam wasn't like Eric in that sense.

Well, duh. Because Cam was *nothing* like Eric. He never had been.

"I think what he did was admirable. Did Royce see everything?"

Serenity frowned. "I don't know. He hasn't said anything to me about it." Royce was pretty good about talking to her about everything. She had assumed he walked out of the auditorium with his friends before Warren started the fight.

"Imagine if he did. What would Cam be teaching him? If he hit the guy, he'd be teaching Royce it's okay to use violence as a means to communicate. If he called the guy names in return, he'd be teaching him it's okay to stoop down to their level. Instead, Cam chose to be the bigger man—because he is—and walked away. He would've taught Royce that engaging is not always the answer. It's okay to not give those kinds of people the attention they want. And we both know that's what that disgusting family wants."

Serenity pulled her lips down into a pout, half laughing. "Why do you have to make so much sense and make me feel even worse about how I acted?"

Opal moved closer and pulled her into a side hug. "Because that's what sisters do for each other. You need to talk to him. The man all but confessed he loved you. That's pretty big. He's amazing, and you will be the biggest idiot if you let him walk away for good."

All true points once again for her annoying sister. Why did she have to be so right?

That was another thing that had her panicking. Cam had confessed he loved her. Her boys too. It had popped out so fluidly that she wasn't even sure he realized he said it.

What did she say back?

That she loved him?

Because she did.

But oh no. She said nothing. She let him walk out like he didn't matter to her.

It all frightened her. She loved Eric in the beginning too, and look how that turned out.

Cam wasn't Eric though. Something she kept forgetting over and over. They were nothing alike.

"I think I screwed up so badly he's never going to forgive me."

"God, you're so dumb sometimes. That man would walk through fire for you. Get your ass dressed and go to him. Now."

Serenity threw her hand at the oven. "I'm cooking a turkey."

"That you most likely screwed up. What do you know about cooking a turkey?"

"I followed the instructions."

"Yeah, okay." Opal pushed Serenity toward the exit. "I'll finish the turkey. You go get Cam so he can enjoy this beautiful meal together with us." Opal's brows rose, her gaze stern. "Now."

"Fine." Serenity huffed as she walked out of the kitchen.

She knew her sister was right. It didn't make it easier for her. Despite it being late afternoon, she was still in her PJs. They were comfy, and why bother getting dressed when she and the boys weren't going anywhere? But of course, she couldn't show up looking like a rag doll when she had a lot of groveling to do.

After throwing on a pair of jeans and a white sweater that accentuated her curves and swiping a small amount of makeup on, she was ready to leave. Too bad her nerves were jumping off the charts. The drive was painful because at every turn she wanted to flip the car in the other direction. He would not want to see her. Not after what she said to him —or the lack of words as well. Hell, he probably wasn't even home. It was Christmas Eve.

Eyeing his truck in the driveway when she pulled in said this was happening no matter how much it terrified her. The other vehicle in the driveway told her she should go home and do this another day. He had company. He wouldn't want to be bothered by her.

Then Opal's stern voice popped into her head, and she knew if she didn't at least try, her sister would do something crazy, like drive her back over here herself.

She tried the house first, coming to the conclusion he was in the workshop when nobody answered.

Even though she knew she could walk right in. She knocked instead, waiting for him to answer the door.

His brother opened it in his place.

"Well, someone finally came to their senses. Glad it was you. My brother still hasn't found his. Not that I think he was wrong. But he is an idiot for not trying to work it out. Anyway, you hurt my brother again and I will destroy you. Come on in." Vin stepped to the side, waving her in with a smile on his face.

She had no idea what to say to his little speech, so she remained silent.

"Yo, bro, I'm leaving. I'll see you tomorrow." Vin swiped his coat from the workbench behind him and then looked at her. "I hope I see you tomorrow as well."

Then he left, closing out the cold wind swirling outside. Yet the room itself remained cold. Or perhaps it was Cam's stoic expression.

She moved closer his way but stayed behind the couch while he stood in front of it. She wasn't sure if he wanted her to come closer. His entire body language spoke volumes. Rigid stance, dead expression, closed fists.

"I didn't mean to interrupt you two. I could come back."

"He has a date tonight. He was leaving soon anyway."

A date? On Christmas Eve? That made her curious, but not enough to ask.

"I don't know where to start, so I'll just say I'm sorry. I was out of line, and I shouldn't have said what I did."

Cam sighed, his body finally relaxing. "I'm sorry too. I never want you to think I don't care, but I also don't want to overstep where I shouldn't."

"Oh, Cam, I know how much you care. I was an idiot. You were right. I was subconsciously comparing you to Eric and I should've never done that. He left me high and dry so many times. I've been fighting so many things all my life raising those boys on my own. Here this asshole is attacking one of my boys, and I felt all alone again, even with you standing right next to me. But I shouldn't assume you'll know that I want you standing by my side when it comes to them. To be clear, I do. If we're going to make this work, I want to be a team. In everything. Even the boys. They need someone like you in their life. A good role model."

"Just so you know, I did want to hit him."

Serenity walked around the couch and placed her hand on his chest. His heart was beating like crazy, matching the tune of her own. "And you showed more willpower than most do. That's the kind of man I want my sons to emulate. I'm sorry I didn't see that on my own. Opal pointed that out to me. Because yeah, I didn't understand why you wouldn't stick up for yourself. But I get it now. You were. With more strength than I've ever seen. I'm so sorry I didn't come sooner. I was scared. I still am."

Cam put his hand over hers resting on his chest. "I'm scared too. Life can be scary. But I want to wade through it all with you. Because I love you."

No more holding back. She couldn't. He was right once again.

"I love you too."

She could feel her entire body vibrating with nerves.

One of Cam's hands smoothed a path down her side until it found her hip, pulling her closer. His other one grasped hers and pulled it to his mouth, bestowing a soft kiss to it. His sweet touch calmed her down as it always did. He centered her.

"I never thought I'd hear those words from you. I had hoped so, but I never actually envisioned it happening." Then his lips were covering hers, his tongue diving in, and she knew she was truly home.

Him. Her. They were perfect for each other. She was only sorry it took her so long to see it. To recognize it.

The coldness she had felt moments before dissipated as his sweet kisses and caresses warmed her up.

They came up for air, both breathing heavily, their hearts still beating in an erratic tune together.

"I'm making a turkey. Opal is finishing it while I'm here. Would you like to join us tonight? The boys have missed you as much as I have."

"I would love that." His eyes glided to the sleigh behind her. "Can we do something before we leave?"

A bright smile built on her face as she looked at the sleigh. "You wanna go for a ride?"

"I do, very much."

She pulled on his hand and headed for the sleigh. "Then let me take you on one. This present is starting to become my favorite one ever."

Cam helped her up in the sleigh, then sat down and pulled her onto his lap. "It's definitely one of my favorites."

She hadn't appreciated the gift in the beginning, but she loved it now. Loved him. She proceeded to show him how much as the heat built so high between them, they could've burst into flames.

15

New Year's Eve

THE DOOR SHUT QUIETLY, then a loud whoop rented the air as Cam picked her up from behind and twirled her.

"I don't know if I'm more excited we're about to start a new year and I can't wait to see what that entails or if I'm more excited we have the entire house to ourselves tonight."

Serenity turned around in his arms, kissing him thoroughly and lavishly on the lips. That had to be a good answer to his question.

"How about both," she whispered against his lips as her hands trailed down, grabbing his ass, pulling him into her. He was hard as a rock, and her body was already humming a delicious tune.

"You're right. Both things are very exciting. Did they grab a charger for their phones? In case they need to call us."

She chuckled, cupping his face. "I made sure Royce and Randall each grabbed one. They will be fine. It's only for the night at their friend's house, who they have known since they were five. There's nothing to worry about."

Cam swooped her up into his arms, surprising her once again, eliciting another delighted squeal from her lips. He sat down on the couch with her cradled in his arms. She didn't have a fireplace, but one would've been nice right about now. It would add to the coziness she was currently feeling.

"I'll have you know, I worry all the time about you three when I'm not with you. Now that I can vocalize my worry about them even more to you, I can't help myself. It's been snowing all day and it's picking up. You know how the roads can get."

"They promised to text me when they get to the house." She rubbed his cheek. "I love how much you worry about them like their own father should. You don't know what that means to me."

She knew he didn't fully understand how much it meant. Tonight she could tell him. And give him the present he truly deserved. Considering she had wallowed in pity that was uncalled for almost a whole week before Christmas, she never did end up buying him a gift. So when they went to his parents' house on Christmas Day, he was the only one who didn't get anything from her. No one had seemed to notice, and Cam assured her he already got what he wanted.

But it wasn't okay, and she stressed about it the past few days, until yesterday when the light bulb went off. It blinked so brightly, it almost blinded her that she was doing something completely insane.

"So what do you want to do all night? Stay up until midnight and ring in the new year? Find a party to crash? Go to bed early?" He wiggled his eyebrows playfully as a naughty grin touched his lips.

"A mixture of that. Go to bed early and ring the new year in there."

"Oh, I like the sound of that."

Considering it was only six o'clock, they had a long time until midnight rolled around.

"Snacks first."

She hopped up from his lap before he could trap her, and she knew he wanted to. She could see it in his eyes the things he wanted to do to her. Not that she was opposed to any of it. Bring. It. On. Her body was screaming for the attention.

But she had to get her present out of the way first or it'd consume her all night if she didn't.

"That nacho dip I saw you making earlier? You don't have to ask me twice."

He stood up, but she put a hand on his chest to stop him. A frown melted on his lips.

"Sit." She blew out a breath, then forced a smile out. "Please. Sit. I have something for you first, and then we can eat, celebrate, and have lots and lots of sex tonight."

Hopefully.

As long as he liked his present.

"You didn't have to get me anything. Are you still stressing about Christmas? I have everything I want or need. Whatever it is, I don't need it."

"Maybe. But I want to give it to you. I *need* to give it to you."

She couldn't be certain because she knew the sleigh had been a sore spot between them at first, but she figured he put a lot of love and effort into it. No. She knew he had. It was in the details. The sleigh was still sitting in his workshop. It couldn't stay in there because eventually he'd need the room for other projects. They'd work out together where to put it. Somewhere only they could enjoy it. Because it was their special place. She didn't want anyone else ruining it for them. Though the boys saw it a few days ago when they hung out at Cam's place. They loved it, of course. Cam had told her on the sly he had cleaned and sanitized it before they got there, suspecting the boys would want to see it. She let them ooh and aah over it for a few minutes then ushered them out. It felt too weird for her to see them lingering around it when all her memories concerning it were very naughty ones.

What she was about to give him, she put a lot of love and effort into as well. It wasn't as beautiful and elegant as his, but she tried her best—for a novice.

Cam nodded and sat back, relaxing into the couch. "Okay. Give it to me."

Now that it was time, she hesitated. Dreaded it like everything she finally had in her grasp would be ripped away for good.

"Serenity—"

"Be right back." Then she left the room before he could stop her.

She had to snap out of her nervousness. Everything would turn out well. He loved her. She loved him. She hadn't been this happy in a very long time. She hadn't even been this happy with Eric.

She walked back into the living room with the present. A long, rectangular item wrapped in Christmas paper that had dancing Santas on it.

Cam chuckled when he saw the paper, the same thing he did when he saw her dump out the presents at his parents' house. It was amusing and cute and the reason she bought it. It was one thing that didn't make her want to puke about the holiday. And she knew her grandma would've gotten a kick out of it, and that made her smile as well.

Maybe she'd learn to enjoy the holiday again. Remembering the good times about her was better than remembering the one horrible day that was hard to erase from her memory. They all grieved in their own way. Her mom—and most of the rest of the family—tried to make Christmas even cheerier. Hiding their pain. In essence, they did what she did. Faked it like it didn't bother them. But it was time to stop that. She had to deal with her grief and enjoy the holiday once again. If not for herself, then for her boys.

"I'm guessing it's a sign." He chuckled, his finger diving under the side where the tape was located.

That was a good guess. Hopefully, he didn't freak out when he saw what it said.

She tentatively sat down as the wrapping paper floated to the floor. He remained silent as he stared at the wooden sign she had created yesterday afternoon. She even had a few nicks and scrapes on her hands that he hadn't noticed yet.

If she hadn't reached out to Mase for help, she knew she couldn't have accomplished it on her own. She had no idea how to work with wood. But he had made her something out of the thing he loved most. She wanted to give him something back like that in return.

"Serenity..." he whispered, his eyes glued to the sign.

What did that mean?

Because only two answers could be given. Yes or no. She had painstakingly carved out the simple question, "Will you marry me?" She had even given the piece of wood a lovely decorative border. She thought about staining it, but Mase stopped her. He told her Cam would love it like this. Considering Mase helped with what she wrote on it, she had high hopes she'd get the answer she wanted.

He finally looked up, reached forward, wrapping his hand around her neck, and pulled her closer. His lips attacked hers, telling her with the frenzied kiss how much he liked his present.

"Yes. A thousand times yes. But are you sure?" He rested his forehead against hers, his warm hand still holding her firmly behind the neck. "We can take this relationship slowly. A few weeks ago, you wanted only sex. I don't want to rush you into anything. Hell, I was ready to ask this question months ago. That's how long I've loved you."

She kissed him softly, then straightened. His hand dropped to her waist and his eyes glittered with happiness, yet a touch of trepidation.

"I'm sorry it took me so long to see how wonderful you are. How much you have loved me for so long. I know this isn't the best gift, but I wanted you to know how much I love you and the support you always show me and the boys. I'm ready for everything. For you in our lives every day, all day. Supporting me. Supporting them. Doing everything as a team. So when Sharon or some other bitch tries to go at me and my sons, I have backup. Or at least someone to hold me back since you're the lover not the fighter in this family."

A boisterous laugh left his mouth. "I'll make sure my wife doesn't get herself arrested."

She bit her bottom lip, trying to hold in her smile, but she couldn't do it. His wife. Oh, how she loved the sound of that.

"Did you make this?" He looked at the sign again, brushing his hands across parts of it.

"I know it's amateurish, but I tried. Mase helped me. I

have the wounds to prove it." She held up her hands to show the nicks and scrapes.

He grabbed them, kissing each wound he saw.

"We're hanging this up. It's the best present I've ever received."

Her smile brightened even more. That's all she had hoped for.

"Now we have even more to look forward to this new year. A wedding, a move, starting our lives together."

He kissed her again, moving the sign to the coffee table so he could pull her into his lap. "I can't wait. Whatever you want for any of it. I'm game."

"I don't want a big wedding. Something small and intimate. We can move into your house. That workshop is like your home too, and I'd never take that away from you. And the sleigh can stay hidden in your backyard away from prying eyes."

He saw the twinkle in her eyes, getting the drift of her meaning.

"I do have a few neighbors, even if they aren't right next to me. They might see stuff."

"It's a pretty big sleigh. And I have a soon-to-be husband who is good with his hands. I'm sure he can figure something out for the privacy aspect."

"I am good with my hands." He winked.

Then he proceeded to show her just how well-versed his hands could be.

DID YOU READ THE FIRST BOOK IN THIS HEARTWARMING HOLIDAY SERIES? CHECK OUT MERRY ME!

For Elliot & Lynn's Story
MERRY ME
A Holiday Romance Novel, #1

He never knew a simple gift left on his porch step would mend his wounded heart.

Hiding his dislike for the holidays isn't easy, especially when Chief Elliot Duncan meets a woman who captures his attention with one sweet smile. Lynn Carpenter is beautiful, strong-willed, and hardworking, and he doesn't know how to return her gift that was left on his porch by mistake. As Christmas approaches, it doesn't take much for the holiday spirit to seep in, not when Lynn makes it so effortless with her excitement. The only thing he wants for Christmas this year is her heart. But between his meddling father and the need to take care of her, something she passionately resists, he knows it won't be that simple. He's up for the challenge, because losing Lynn is unacceptable.

FOR AIDEN & THERESA'S STORY
MISTLETOE MAGIC
A HOLIDAY ROMANCE NOVEL, #2

A mistletoe. A kiss. This just might be the start of a beautiful Christmas.

Theresa might not make the best pot of coffee in town, but people still flock to the diner for a cup, even Officer Crowl, who rarely displays a smile since his fiancé died. She'll never be able to win his heart, but it's hard to resist him, especially when he kisses her under the mistletoe. Well, on the cheek, but that has to count for something...right?

Staying busy keeps Officer Aiden Crowl sane. Because when he's idle or alone, he thinks, and nothing good comes from that. Everyone thinks he's the perfect man. They think he's broken because she's gone. He is, just not for the reason they believe. Every time he walks into the diner, one sweet smile from Theresa erases some of the pain. He should stay away from her. Far away. But what is he supposed to do when they're standing under a mistletoe? Kiss her, of course.

FOR BENTLEY & EMMA'S STORY
CHRISTMAS WISH
A HOLIDAY ROMANCE NOVEL, #3

What if you had one wish granted for Christmas? What would it be?

Acting reckless isn't something Bentley Wilson is known for, but when he runs back into a burning building to save a little girl's puppy after specifically told not to do so, that's exactly how most of the town sees him, especially the fire chief who insists he has to help with the annual Christmas party because of his behavior. Throw in the fact the woman he's pined over for too long is getting married, this holiday is going to go down as one of the worst. Until he meets Emma Brookes. She's feisty, headstrong, and holds so much pain hidden in the depths of her beautiful green eyes. He wants nothing more than to erase her sadness. But it's already a season of disaster, and every time they're together, they spar like two warriors dueling to the death. Despite that, he likes the challenge, the crazy way she makes him feel. Before the holiday is over, he vows to get his one Christmas wish. That she never leaves his side.

For James & Erin's Story
Snowed in Love
A Holiday Romance Novel, #4

A blizzard. A cabin. A cup of hot chocolate.
The perfect mixture to fall in love.

James Brennen is nothing but a screwup. At least, in the small town of Mulberry, that's what everyone thinks of him. As a recovering alcoholic, he's trying his best to turn his life around, to be a better man. All of his hard work comes crashing down when he's fired from his job at the hospital—accused of stealing drugs. Nothing ever changes and he's done trying to prove himself. Needing time alone, his friend's cabin in the middle of the woods provides the perfect escape. He knows he's found deep trouble, not only when he gets stranded during a brutal snowstorm, but that he's stuck with the one woman he's wanted since the first day he laid eyes on her. The passion burns bright between them, but it doesn't matter, because as soon as Christmas is over, he's leaving for good.

FOR MASE & HOPE'S STORY
HOLIDAY HOPE
A HOLIDAY ROMANCE NOVEL, #6

Let the merriment begin...Operation Holiday Hope commence.

Life hasn't been the same since she quit her job working for the tyrant mayor, but Hope Bronson is trying her best. She's attempting to embrace the holiday spirit and pretend she's happy when, in reality, she feels stuck in a rut. And why? She can't even explain it to herself, let alone to anyone else, without risking being called a drama queen. And men... don't even get her started. Talk about bad choices every. Single. Time. Except...maybe one guy, but she can't trust her own judgment. It doesn't matter that everyone tells her he's a good one. She's leery of opening herself up to another bad decision—unless he can convince her otherwise.

Mase Brandt can't believe his luck when he's asked to fix a Nativity scene for the church. The one and only woman to steal his heart with ease works there. A few months ago, she shut him out with little fanfare. This time, he's not giving up so easily. The holidays are a joyous time of year. He'll use anything and everything to his advantage to win her heart. He knows she won't make a moment of it easy on him. But that's okay. He has a few tricks up his sleeve. Let the festivities begin.

ABOUT THE AUTHOR

I'm a *USA Today* Bestselling Author that loves to write contemporary romance and romantic suspense novels, although I am partial to romantic suspense. I even dabble in paranormal. Honestly, I love anything that has to do with romance. As long as there's a happy ending, I'm a happy camper. And insta-love...yes, please! I love baseball (Go Twins!) and creating awesome crafts. I graduated with a Bachelor's Degree in Criminal Justice, working in that field for several years before I became a stay-at-home mom. I have a few more amazing stories in the works. If you would like to learn more about me and my books, head to my website by scanning the QR code. Thanks for reading!

Scan me